The  :

An ordinary family holiday to France becomes almost unbelievable for four children. An action packed adventure

By

Jack Emson

To Dewi and Gwennan

Martin Fut

ox £3.49
40

Acknowledgements

Jacob Frost's help in my understanding of the English
language and grammar stuff like
Sue Evans for her sterling crossing of I's & t's and
speeling
Chris Frost for the jacket design
The Welsh Book Council

This book is dedicated to the real Four

And of course ….Mrs. F.

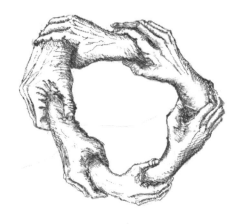

The Four

By

Jack Emson

Foreword

This is the first of a series of stories following the four Fielding children. It is a journey and I hope you have some fun going on it. I ought to say right now that 'Jack Emson' is a pseudonym or writing name for Mark Frost. It appears that there is a pretty successful author by that name but I'm the one who lives in south Wales and who's played a bit of cricket and strangely enough has a family not too dissimilar to the one in this story. So 'Jack Emson' it is after members of my family, notably my Grandfather. All the places are real and I'd recommend going to them all some time.

All Quotations are from the works of Marcus Aurelius

© Mark Frost 2008

Published in 2012 by New generation Publishing

First Edition

The author asserts the moral right under the Copyright, Designs and Patents Act 1988 to be identified as the author of this work.

All references to persons either named or otherwise, be they real or fictional is entirely unintentional!

All Rights reserved. No part of this publication may be reproduced, stored in a retrieval system or transmitted, in any form or by any means without the prior consent of the author, nor be otherwise circulated in any form of binding or cover other than that which it is published and without a similar condition being imposed on the subsequent purchaser.

www.newgenerationpublishing.info

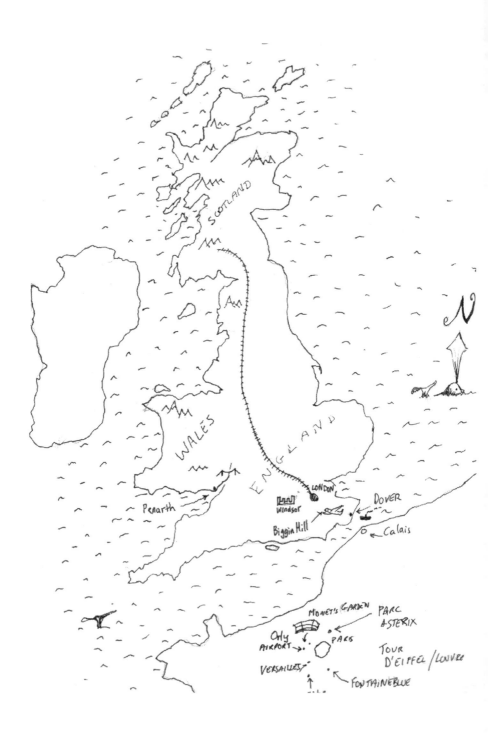

Chapters &Titles

Chapter One

<u>A Christmas Eve party</u>

December 24th

The boy rubbed clear a patch from the steamed up window and looked through its watery glass down along the short road. It was Christmas Eve and, much to Nathan's approval, it was snowing.

'These are serious flakes', he thought, 'as big as baubles and they're sticking'. He could see the visitors' footprints quickly merging back to white smoothness. The cars at the end of the close, on the main road, slowly sludged along, their headlamps searching out the vagueness of kerbs, their tyres leaving furrows. The hurrying flakes, brought pools of colour to streetlights casting a dull orange glow over this quiet cul de sac in the small coastal Welsh town of Penarth.

Nathan went to turn back to the Christmas Eve party behind him but something caught his eye. He quickly rubbed at the window again, pressing against the glass. His eyes widened as he saw a black Mercedes scream round the corner where his close joined the main road, skidding at speed and accelerating towards him, spewing slush from the rear wheels.

Its driver parked immediately behind an old brown camper van with blacked out windows. A man got out and looked around. Eight year old Nathan moved quickly away from his lounge window, so as not to be seen. After a few seconds, he peeked out past a large stuffed Father Christmas to see a man, with silver hair and a stretched face wearing a long black cloak and a black hat. The figure climbed into the camper van and dragged out its occupant. Nathan had never seen anyone in the strange van. What was difficult to see in the falling snow, was clear to see in the car's tracks. Something heavy was being pulled towards the boot of the Mercedes.

'That will cost loads to fix,' he thought, noticing that the boot didn't shut properly. It was badly crumpled and the lights were smashed. Ignoring the party going on, Nathan turned, ran, around to the front door and stepped out into the snow wearing his father's shoes. He hid behind the drain pipe. A furious sound made him look back towards the main road, as a silver car took the same bend at breakneck speed and accelerated like a bullet towards the van. He couldn't believe how damaged the silver car was. The nose was completely destroyed; one headlight was missing with the other pointing sideways like a one eyed crab. The second thing that impressed him was that the car was an Aston Martin, he'd only ever seen one once before.

The black Mercedes began to pull out to leave, but having seen the silver car approaching, it suddenly veered into the middle of the road at speed. This sent the Aston Martin skidding into a neighbour's front garden and shooting two plumes of muddy snow all over the house, before it turned to chase the leaving Mercedes. The two cars now raced, one in pursuit of the other, taking the corner onto the main road and causing chaos.

"Nathan!" shouted his Dad from the lounge. Nathan returned inside, amazed at what he had seen. He couldn't believe it let alone understand it. What he could understand though, was that the Christmas Eve party was being run badly by his eccentric father who was now unveiling his latest invented game. Nathan knew it was rubbish and his older sister Laura and brothers Jacob, and Matthew looked wearily at him as he went back in.

He could tell that the guests were only politely laughing and glanced across to Laura. He could see that she was desperate to lift the party.

His twelve year old sister suddenly decided to do something about it. She grabbed her three brothers, pulling them into the kitchen. The aroma of mulled wine and the remains of a roast dinner, half finished chocolate puddings gently illuminated by the multi coloured Christmas lights, provided a mellow atmosphere.

"Boys, what are we going to do? Dad's losing the plot completely, everyone's bored."

"Yeah I know! No-one's interested, let's do something" said Jacob. Nathan was desperate to tell them what he had seen, but was interrupted by Matthew, the youngest of the four.

"I know!" he said, cupping a hand to his sister's ear and whispering something.

"Oh, yeah" Laura's face brightened up and she ran out of the kitchen and then up the stairs. Matthew walked into the lounge and stood in the middle of the guestsand appealed;

"Can we do the holiday game, Dad?" Laura heard Matthew's question knowing it would stop her father because it was a major tradition for the Fielding family. She visualised the metal globe, the sort that she imagined might be found in a dusty old library or a stately home. It was very old and large with specially raised bits to represent the Himalayas and the Alps.

Laura opened the loft door, flicked the switch for light. Most of the glow was blocked by large mattresses, cots and boxes of what she thought was rubbish. She crept along, brushing off a few cobwebs on the way until she reached a dark corner, grabbed the globe and smiled. Here it was!

'This must be over 100 years old' she thought, noticing three clear finger prints in the dust gathered on its top, but thinking nothing of it. Alongside the globe was an old trunk which had been left open. Laura had never seen it before and looked inside. There she found, amongst a pile of what seemed to be old rubbish, a leather-bound booklet. She picked it up. The book's covers were curled with age and the leather had stiffened.

Laura was pleased to be bringing the globe into the lounge and to much applause (and relief) it was positioned in front of the fire.

"What's this all about?" inquired Mr. McDermott, an old Irish friend of the family with a smile the size of Belfast. He was answered by Nathan.

"Well, you are blindfolded and then oneach family's turn to spin the globe, wherever your finger points, that's where you are supposed take your next holiday."

Jacob was in charge and announced to the nervous contenders.

"Ladies and Gentlemen, from the people that brought you…"

"Jacob get on with it" interrupted Laura

"And now the moment you've been waiting for" Jacob continued, "the time has come. Let the games begin!"

The McDermotts volunteered to go first. They poised as the old globe whirred and creaked as it spun. After much laughter and drawn out deliberation, Mrs. McDermott was given a second turn having landing on the Iraq - Iran border. This was largely due to Mr. McDermott cheating and clearly not taking the game seriously. Having spun again, the replacement of Arizona was received with much applause and apparently a dream come true.

"We can't challenge you again as it will hold up proceedings" announced Jacob impatiently. "Go on Mum, your turn."

"Yes go on Mrs. F," said Mr. Fielding. The mother of the four children took her turn and put on the customary blindfold. The globe spun round emitting a grinding noise on its ancient and rusty axis. All went quiet. The globe spun on. Faces watched as continents whizzed by, oceans came and went.

"Now Mum," shouted Jacob on several occasions all ignored by his mother.

"The Antarctic is good in August," shouted Mr McDermott who received a smack from his wife.

The finger of Mrs. F. stopped the globe over France and on lifting it away; the area uncovered was Paris. She was overjoyed and there was much celebrating. Everyone joined in the cheering and Jacob started arather early Christmas Eve versions of *Auld Lang Syne*, *Frère Jacques* and *Vive La France*. Nathan took advantage of the distraction slipped out to the front door again.

'What's that?' wondered Matthew, looking at the window and seeing a silver car drive up. He went outside to the front door and joined Nathan.

"I saw that silver car before Matt, but now it's really muddy.

"Who's that getting out and what's the grey van doing? It's been there ages!" Matthew noticed a gash on the driver's forehead and one arm hanging limply at his side. He looked at his brother,

"Come on let's tell the others".

Back inside, as much as he tried, Matt was completely ignored by the 'others'. 'Little Matt' as he was known, looked disappointed. No one listened to him, even his Mum, as he was the youngest and six years old. His Father appeared,

"Now then, off to Bedfordshire" he said. Matthew sank his head on his father's neck and agreed. Nathan watched them go upstairs and thought about the injuries to the driver of the Aston Martin.

Fresh snow and the excitements of Christmas Day came and went. Presents were opened, dinner eaten, visitors seen and just when the family was flagging, Mrs F. walked in to the lounge holding a large pile of brochures.

"Let's have a holiday meeting. I've got guides and instructions for driving in France, including reminders to keep on the right."

"What now?" grumbled Laura, "A bit keen aren't you?"

"So where are we going on holiday then?"asked Nathan.

Everything went quiet for a few seconds whilst his family stared at him in amazement, exasperated and annoyed.

"Nathan," everyone shouted.

"Don't you ever listen to anything?" asked Laura.

"Oh well, I do but I thought we were planning next week for school…" but Nathan was interrupted again.

"Yeah like we need to know when the Eiffel Tower opens in January so we can pop up after school," Jacob laughed. Laura joined in.

"I'll need my passport for some top secret spying missions tonight as I plan my geography homework!"

"Oh Mum," Nathan responded with a large lower lip. An argument broke out between the others.

"Well if you have nothing better to do than argue, I suggest that you all write out a packing list so that we're ready for our departure," announced Mrs. F.

"Departure?" said Laura, rather annoyed "It's only a holiday to France, sounds like we are leaving for good".

"I wish you were" added Jacob

"Now then you lot" piped his mother.

"I know, I can use my new rucksack I had for Christmas on holiday," enthused Nathan.

"Yes that's one reason we bought it for you" said his mother.

"Yeah it's great and has some cool pockets and secret sections in it and it's really comfortable even when it's loaded up."

Laura looked up from the computer, "It's only a bag".

Nathan walked off towards the window and looked out at the parked cars down the street and the grey van again. Forgetting the others, he went up to his room and drew out the new bag from under his bed. He looked at it, holding it up. 'It's a good bag whatever the others say' he thought 'and I can fit all sorts of thing in it.' He was pleased with this and was sure he would use it some time.

Slightly bored, Laura went to make a call on the phone to her friend Maddy. Just before Maddy's father had handed over the phone, Laura made out a strange sound on the line, but on hearing her ecstatic friend, forgot about it until the final Christmas 'goodbyes' were said and the click sound came again. On returning to the others, she looked puzzled.

"What's up Laura?" asked Matthew.

"Oh well, when I got through to Maddy there were lots of click sounds and the call seemed a bit echoed".

"Maybe she was typing on her laptop?"

Laura's puzzled face went un-noticed by the others as excitement grew about how long it would take to climb the Eiffel Tower!

Jacob started singing a TV advert jingle in a faked American accent, then addressed his father in german as "Vater" with the emphasis on the german 'f' sound. He launched himself at Nathan and Matthew and then, eventually, his father who all ended up in a bundle on the floor.

"So I take it we are finished then?" said an annoyed Mrs. F. "I see that the males have decided to revert to playground banter and games. Meeting finished at 20:46."

"What do you expect mum?" said Laura. She moved across to the lounge bay window and looked out. In the cold winter's night and down the shared drive her view adjusted to the old grey van and what seemed to be a person leaving it from the far side. She couldn't be certain of course; it could have just been someone passing by....

Chapter Two

<u>**The journey begins**</u>

Eight months later.......... August 1ˢᵗ

Nathan looked out of his bedroom window and across the fields beyond the garden. He noticed how so many things were ready, flowers in bloom, trees in full leaf, lawns dried up. He thought how busy the end of term had been with summer festivals, end of term concerts, discos and best of all, the beginning of the school holidays. At last, the term was completed, the school year finished and of course.....

"Packing for holiday," shouted Mrs F.

The packing preparations had gone reasonably well. Laura and her parents had been busy, but when Mrs. F. asked the boys what they had done…. Nathan knew that the boys had done nothing.

"Nothing!" Mrs. F. Shouted. She stomped up to the boy's room and started to give a good half hour lecture to the boys on their 'slothfulness and the virtues of personal responsibility'. Laura and her Father kept a low profile, struggling to stop giggling and feeling smug. Laura's bag was neatly organised, clothes folded correctly and allocated according to the time they would be away.

"Right then, are we ready to go?" she asked impatiently.

Finally the car was packed, the TV recorder set, the cats and rabbits feeding catered for. All six boarded the car and finally, set off. Down the short cul-de-sac, past the usual cars, an old grey van which hadn't moved for ages, several neighbors gardening and walking dogs, right onto the main road, past Cosmeston Lakes Park, on through Penarth and away on holiday.

The car picked up speed and slipped onto the orange lit motorway. The ribbon of three lanes zoomed smoothly out of Cardiff around Newport, past the shores of the Bristol Channel and onto the mighty strutting towers of the Second Severn crossing, a festival of cables and suspension.

The motorway now lost any interest for the Four as more dark miles slipped by into the night. Jacob's stomach rumbled. He called from the rear seats,

"Can we stop at the next motorway service station for chicken and chips?" His request was successful and a meal was bought. After the boys had been scolded for throwing chips in Laura's hair and when greasy fingers had been cleaned and toilets visited, they returned to the car. As his father turned on the engine, Jacob called out

"Where's Nathan?"

"He's not here," replied Matthew.

"Not again," moaned Laura "he's got lost everywhere else, a motorway services is a first even for him".

"I saw him in the loo," said Jacob who set off and searched the gents drawing some surprised looks from travellers as he checked all the cubicles, but no eight year old boy was to be found.

The shop was empty. Running back to the car, Jacob joined his Father and Mrs. F who was now panicking like a bewildered chicken. He could see that she was thinking the worst.

The toilet door was smooth and very high, especially for someone who was four foot tall. Standing on the toilet seat and reaching up was pointless. Crawling under into the next cubicle was impossible and, given the state of the floor, a no brainer. The loo-roll holder was too smooth to grip onto, even with rubber soled trainers. Worst of all, the lock was still stuck. Nathan was at first, confused. He had slid the bolt across himself on entering the cubicle but hadn't felt it stick or jam. Even forcing the bolt with a well aimed karate kick was useless. He immediately felt isolated. He knew that no-one was in the men's loo when he entered and worried that no one would hear him.

"Dad…? Mum?"Nothing.

He started to bite his lip.

"Dad….? Anyone?"Nothing

Then he heard footsteps, but they appeared to move away rather than come towards him. 'Had that person been there all the time?' he wondered. The walls of the toilet appeared to grow.

'Had the others driven off without him? Who was the person who had been in the loo and hadn't answered him?' But then the steps returned quite quickly now and rushed up to the cubicle door. Nathan panicked and cowered back into the corner of the loo fearing an attack from anywhere. He looked up and under the door but his eyes kept returning to the bolt expecting the door to open any moment. Nathan's heart pumped hard, he breathed quickly, gripped the top of the cistern and brought it towards him as a shield.

The bolt slowly opened and then ….nothing. The steps that had sprinted back to him now disappeared at a similar pace. He waited and waited and then slowly pushed at the door. It opened out to reveal an empty room. He walked out looking around at every angle. More footsteps. He stepped back into the cubicle, but this time it was a cleaner who sloppily dropped his bucket on the floor and began his routine mopping.

He was an old man but seemed ok to Nathan.

"Alright lad?" the cleaner asked.

"Oh er yeah" Nathan lied and walked out.

Eventually, a few minutes later, Nathan walked onto the concourse and met, to his great relief, the rest of the family. He found it difficult to describe what had happened as his mother engulfed him.

"Oh Nathan we were so worried" she gushed.

"So," said Laura as they resumed the journey and the car rejoined the M4, "how come the lock was stuck and then it wasn't?" This was a very good question which Nathan couldn't answer because he wasn't sure how it suddenly became freed up. He thought no-one would believe him and the sequence of events, so after a while he kept quiet. The rest of the journey was uneventful for him other than watching the night skies of Heathrow with brightly lit planes taking off and landing.

What no-one had realised while they were travelling was that they had been followed all the way by a sleek, black car.

Mrs. F's sister's house had been chosen for a stopover in Surrey before catching an early ferry. The house sat quietly in a small suburban road in Cheam. Nathan looked up at the front. He was surprised by the fact that it was mostly covered with scaffolding, though he couldn't see any building works. They were greeted by fifteen friendly cats, since their masters were on holiday. Everyone went straight to a bed that had been kindly left ready by Auntie Rosie. Nathan settled down in a sleeping bag, got out his torch from his new backpack and started reading. He struggled to concentrate, still thinking about that incident and how scared he had felt.

August 2nd

    The little Jacob could remember of his history lessons that year were about the Second World War. He saw the welcome to Dover sign and looked at the white-cliffed ferry port, which was bright and busy. The chalk-lined coast that had welcomed wave after wave of heroes fresh from the Battle of Britain, now beckoned the family as the car snaked over the Downs. He watched the vast, impressive sea-going ferries come and go in silent obedience to their tiny, unseen human masters. Winding through queues of cars and checkpoints, the car eventually boarded the ferry, parked on deck 5a and everyone climbed up narrow steps, queued up with lots of others and eventually sat down to a welcome breakfast. The floating carrier moved off slowly and steadily into the channel.

    After breakfast, Nathan asked to go to the top of the ferry.

    "Good call Nath," said his father "the weather's pleasant, the sun's warm and the sea air invigorating." When the call came to rejoin cars there was quite a crowding and bustling of people pouring into the entrance doors from the sun deck. What seemed like a scuffle took place deep in the crowd. Two men grappled with each other and one shoved Nathan out of the way, much to the annoyance of those nearby. Nathan had became separated yet again and called out "Mum, Dad", but as much as his parents tried to get to him, the pack of dense crowd forced them apart. An elbow knocked him to the floor and he winced in pain. A man grabbed at him, he thought to help him. Nathan looked up. This man reeked of cigarettes, had a deep guttural cough and greasy grey hair. He also noticed that he was missing a middle finger on one hand. This hand grasped Nathan's ear and hair but couldn't quite hold him as he rolled away into the marching feet and legs of hundreds of travellers returning to their cars. The man lunged at Nathan again who could smell his breath as he got close, but somehow Nathan wasn't held firm. Quite how Nathan did not know as he was powerless. He crawled to a corner between the doors and wall of the deck stairs, hoping that the mass of feet would protect him from any further attack.

After a few more worrying minutes, when the returning crowds had finally got to the car decks, he looked up and, despite his tears, was relieved as his father pulled him up out of the corner. The family all joined up on the top deck.

"Daydreaming again Nathan?" scolded his mother.

"Oh but no! I was pushed away and again someone tried to get me…"

"Of course," she replied sarcastically, "this had better not happen again." He looked away, still upset by that man in the crowd and that no one would believe him. He watched the wake of the waves churn, snow-like, then he looked back to all that was known and familiar before facing forward to look out for a new country and a new adventure.

Chapter Three

<u>Foreign soil</u>

Out of the rear side window Matthew watched a flock of sea gulls swoop and shriek onto a clump of bacon rashers that seemed to have been thrown into the sea, probably from the ferry kitchen window by a lazy junior chef, or so he thought. Only a few seconds of pecking was enjoyed by the white-backed maritime vultures as a wave crashed over the gulls' booty. Matthew smiled as the lucky meal was cut short by the roaring rattle of chains and a crashing splash created by a vast metal ramp lowered down at the instructions from French voices. The gulls swirled round and caught a thermal, soaring up high. The men took charge as the cars were signalled away by gloved workers. One by one, cars set off for their various adventures. Matthew watched his father nervously following all the other Brits driving on the 'wrong' side of the road.

He looked out of the window again and noticed the crossed out sign of Calais. He didn't understand why it was like that and rested his head against his brother's hoody and slowly slipped away into a dream about being captain of a large ship, which then became a coach travelling through many enormous fields and tree-lined roads. He came to and looked at the car clock; he'd been asleep for four hours. The silver people-carrier had arrived in a small, and what appeared to be a deserted, village where Matthew hoped the gite holiday home was.

Despite reading the sheet that the owners had posted giving travel directions, Matthew could see both of his parents were lost. Jacob called out, "There's the number," and to everyone's relief they spotted a small piece of paper pinned to a tree on the roadside. It said very simply 'nombre 48'.

"Aha Hastings, we have found it!" said Matthew's father who was fond of the odd Agatha Christie who-dunnit novel.

The track alongside was indeed just that, a track, and the car bumped and lumped along this windy route into a forest. It led to a small clearing which forked sharp right to an old farm house. On closer inspection, the house was dank and dark and decidedly dour.

Matthew sensed that the others were disappointed with the old farmhouse before them. He climbed stiffly out of the car with the others as they approached a rusty old gate. The sun appeared to grow darker.

"There's no grass worn by cars," he said. Through the gate they nervously went and then to the front door on which was a most mysterious knocker. Matt was surprised and fascinated by the shape of the knocker which was a combination of six hands all clasped around each other. It seemed as though each were gripping the other tightlyand what was even stranger, it was gold.
"Do you think we should er…?"

His father's sentence was never finished. It was interrupted by a crisp, sharp sound of boots approaching the door, clearly walking along uncovered tiles. Matt knew these weren't any old boots either as they gave the impression of purpose, of military position and of fear. He watched the knocker appear to open, not rotating but almost as if each hand slipped off the other. Slowly, the door creaked wide and in front of them stood a tall figure in black, wearing black gloves

and, as Matthew observed, between his right glove
and the hem of his cloak was not skin but gold
coloured metal. There was a rank smell. He was
struck by the man's face. It seemed stretched,
young and old all at the same time.

He shouted,
"This is bad Dad!"His father completely panicked,
triggering off mass hysteria amongst them all. In
wild retreat the dark figure pursued them, not
quickly, but slowly walking up the track with a
machine like purpose.

Sensing the danger, everyone climbed
frantically into the car while Mr Fielding slammed
it into reverse gear. He drove recklessly through
low clinging branches back to the fork where he
grabbed the hand-brake and produced an alarming,
yet effective, sliding turn. The car slammed its way
down the track, back onto the main road and into
the village.

In this state of mixed shock and silence, the
breathing of six slightly scared souls was all that
could be heard. Laura checked Matthew was ok.
The quietness was broken by thedramatic and
sudden appearance of a motorbiker wearing a lurid
orange crash helmet, white open necked shirt and
jeans. His bike was a celebration of chrome with

wide handlebars and a resonant throaty roar from the engine.

"Hallo" he said with a wide and toothy grin, "You seem to be lost. Can I help?" he added with a pleased and strong french accent.

Laura looked across at her father. She knew this uncalled for help was a surprise to him. He had made it known on the journey that he was not a lover of French motorbikers. She noticed how her mother had warmed to the look of this strong well-built and, she had to accept it, handsome hero upon his majestic charger.

"Well yes, here is the address we need," stammered Mrs F, who Laura thought looked a little flushed.

"I see," said the motorbiker, "pas de probleme, you follow me." This tested Laura's father's recall of his very poor C grade "O" level French. Laura, however, soon prompted him.

"Follow him now Dad." and with that, waiting for no reply, the biker zoomed away, with Mr Fielding desperately keeping up.

White shirt flapping in the wind, the biker took them a mile down the road and pointed to a timid looking French lady clutching keys in front of what was a reassuringly well appointed gite.

Laura's father wound down his window but all he got out was "Tha…" before the biker said, "I know you have had, how you say, a spot of bother, so get in here and any more problems ask for Ivan Furle.". With that he swept, as Laura thought, rather impressively away towards the horizon.

After a whole minute of silence Mrs F said, "Well Hercule Poirot, I'll do the navigation from now on!"

What food had been picked up en-route was laid on a patio table in celebration of their first meal in France. The heavy evening air surrounded and wrapped all six of them in a comforting protection from what had gone on before. No one discussed it, hoping that it hadn't really happened.

"So here we are in France at last," exclaimed a tired Mr Fielding, hiding a yawn.

Later, all slept, quickly and deeply except Laura. Her mind raced before eventually sliding into sleep… 'Where did Ivan Furle come from?.....and the memory of that other man……made her shudder.

Chapter Four

A secret spilled

August 3rd

A cockerel gave out a rather relaxed and non-committed 'cock-a-doo-whatever'. This was followed by another straggly call from a distant cousin. The bedraggled overture woke Jacob who remembered he was in France. He got up and looked out of the boy's bedroom window at the early morning mist. He took a cup of cold water from the wash basin and woke the other two, very effectively.

At breakfast, around the kitchen table, no one could agree what to do.

"Let's go to Fontainebleau," said Mrs. F.

"Fon what?" asked Jacob. Jacob looked at his mother's guide and read out, "Ah yes, the old hunting lodge where previous French Kings, Emperors and their several lady friends, went for holidays to chase deer around....excellent," he said with mock staring eyes and a scowl.

The Palace's grandeur and opulence was clear for all to see. A brown camper van pulled into the next space just as Mrs. F warned Jacob about opening his door onto others. He followed his parents dutifully into what he had to quietly admit was a pretty grand and ornate three sided palace. Whilst inside however, what appeared to him to be a somewhat boring tour for children, turned out to be rather exciting?

Jacob could see his parents listening methodically and predictably on audio headsets to the history, the background to the paintings, the royal parties and births witnessed in each and every room. But then something on the headsets made him look up at the other three. Much to his parent's surprise, it appeared that the children couldn't get enough of the audio tour. Eagerly the four ran from room to room gasping at each other in the excitement and expressing avid interest and surprise from time to time. Their parents were pleased that the four were so rapt by the audio headset history, but Mrs. F. was skeptical.

"One can only get so excited about the minstrel gallery or Louis XV's penchant for hunting," she said to her husband, in full earshot of the four.

At the end of the tour, the family spilled out into the gardens to what was now a slightly mangled picnic. The four children chatted excitedly but would suddenly go quiet when either of the parents was close by. They had all stumbled on an immense secret.

"So what's happening?" asked Matthew who hadn't worked anything out.

"Matt look, for some reason all four of our headsets had been tuned into the wrong frequency so we've overheard some shortwave radio not the boring voice droning on about Louis XV or whatever. It's some people meeting somewhere here in the chateau plotting to steal something very, very famous; butI couldn't catch what it was".

"Something about, well I don't know, sounded like Jackanory" said Jacob, who was itching to get on with things.

"No stupid" said Laura "that was a kids' programme when mum and dad were young. Anyway I don't know what it was, but I know that Fontainbleu Palace is the practice venue for the real thing."

Having joined their parents Matt whispered to Laura,

"Is this thing worth lots of money?"

"Yes…..more than you can imagine, if it's what I think it is."

Chapter Five

The pursuit begins

Laura guessed that because he was so slow and useless, he had to be a poorly paid student. He stood behind a desk, morosely collecting headsets from tourists and Laura noted how he fiddled with his earpieces whilst listening to an i-pod. He was bored. She also noted behind him, at a far desk, a smart suited official fiddling with a lanyard security pass hanging around his neckwho seemed equally unemployed, though frequent calls to and from his cell phone kept him looking busy.

A large contingent of Japanese visitors laughing and chattering noisily stood in front of the four children handing in their headsets. Laura was impatient and her brothers were full of the news of the 'gang'.

"Who's plotting this big robbery?" asked Matt.

"Dunno, but how about we all meet together tonight to piece together the bits of information and work it out?" replied Laura as she began to hand back the audio phones.

"Let's see if we can work out what they are planning to steal," Jacob said and immediately he knew he'd been too loud.

"Jacob!" Laura hissed, but it was too late. She looked across to see the sharply dressed man who suddenly looked up at them and instantly marched over to the student. He took away the four sets that the children had just handed in.

"Quick guys, he knows we know, let's get out" ordered Laura running back to her parents.

"Anything wrong?" asked her mother. Her question was ignored. As the family was edging their way out through the packed crowds, Laura heard desperate adult voices shouting;

"Ou sont les quatre enfants anglais?"

Despite her poor attention to her years even french lessons, Laura could work out that they, the children, were the target. She quickly told the others.

"What's wrong?" asked her father.

"Nothing," said all the four children at once which was an instant giveaway.

"Just stop now!" he demanded. Despite the flow of the crowd, both parents halted the four. The crowd flowed around them like a river past a boulder. "There is something. Why were you in Napoleon's throne room for so long?"

Laura decided that, as the huge exiting crowd was swarming around and since it was deeply embarrassing to have a family conference in such a place, she had to come clean.

"Well, it seems we've over heard a plot about a major robbery and we think they are on to us, "she admitted.

"Oh, of course and who might 'they' be?" replied her father.

"Dad look they are trying to get us" urged Nathan. He didn't need to offer much explanation as five large and angry men were marching towards them. Behind the men and not quite in full eye sight, was the fearsome dark figure that they had seen the previous night.

"Run everyone!"

Three of the men who had been pursuing the family were pinned to a wall, out of sight of the Palace's visitors. The dark tall man in black seemed to have unusual strength as he had all three forced against the wisteria bound wall. The men were unshaven with faces that bore scars of fights and rough living. Their physiques were athletic and strong, yet their master had them in his grip.

"I do not tolerate failure" he rasped at them in french. "One more time like this, will be your last time." The super strong fist that had all three pinned to the wall, squeezed even tighter.

"Monsieur LeClaw," a fourth man came running around the corner holding a scrap of paper. Prompted by this, the fist dropped its hold and three bristly necks fell like pieces of rubbish.

"You'd better have something worthwhile, else…"

"Sir, look!" he showed him the paper "I got the car's registration". He quickly gave this to his master who grasped it in his leather glove. As he squeezed the paper in his glove the leather hem rose up to reveal a sheer metal wrist.

"Ok, so the gang, right, is going to steal a famous painting from the loo." said Laura.

"The Louvre derbrain" replied Jacob.

"You're the derbrain you loser" responded Laura.

"Enough!" barked her mother. "Continue"

"Ok, well the project has got a codename… called Jackanory or something and it's going to happen tomorrow and then they plan to hide in Versailles Palace afterwards."

There was an uncomfortable silence.

"Well?" said Laura "you aren't saying anything!"

"Yeah," added Jacob "you told us to tell you everything and now you look surprised."

"Er you know that Jackanory code name" said his Father. "Well I think you misheard. Jackanory was a children's TV Programme when your Mother and I were children," he looked and gulped at Mrs. F who nodded in agreement, "I think what you've overheard is a plot to steal the most famous painting in the world, it has no value as no one can buy it, but it is priceless. What you mean is the La Joconde or commonly known as the Mona Lisa."The penny dropped, as did all four chins to join Mrs F's.

"Oh yeah we did that at school," said Matthew.

"And it was on Newsround on TV last week, about a big protection thing they were doing for where it's kept," added Nathan.

"No, it's impossible it can't be stolen, it's unthinkable," said Mrs. F "anyway I've planned to go there tomorrow on our itinerary".

"To where?" asked Jacob.

"The Louvre derbrain" answered Laura.

Settling down on his bed, Nathan grabbed a torch from his bag. He replaced the precious present under his bed and read from his book. The cars were driving faster and faster, hunting him, searching out with headlights, tyres squealed looking into each room for him. He ran, the cars burst through the door frame sending splinters around and a tall cloaked man saw him.....

"Nathan, Nathan," said his father "it's just a dream. Shall I tell you a story?"

"Yeah," he said shaking and held his father tightly. His eyes stared into the dark room. "Tell me a Mr Fox story".

One nightmare was gone but he knew, deep down, that another had begun.

Chapter Six

The Louvre

4th August

Early the next morning, a magpie stood on the car's roof-box. Boldly perched up high with its black and white plumage starkly vivid against the dawn mist, it stared at the house. A bedroom window's curtains moved and the bird's beaded black eyes tracked this instantly and altered its stare.

Nathan's face peered out through the window and saw the bird drilling its black eyes into him. The bird screeched as though it was challenging Nathan, lifted its two toned wings and flew up straight at the window. The bird was coming straight to him screeching as it flew, now faster until it virtually hit the window. On contact, it raised its claws, and scraped at the glass slipping like fingernails on a blackboard. The bird composed itself, continuing to stare. Nathan was unnerved by this attack, though he knew he was safe behind the window.

A black Mercedes drove into central Paris, stopped by the bank of the Seine and three men got out, all holding briefcases. Another Mercedes stopped behind the first. Only one man got out this time, wearing a full length black overcoat. He looked up to the sky; hands deep in pockets, walked to the bank and looked up and down the river. He laughed out loud startling a passing jogger, who, having seen his ugly, scarred and stretched face, stepped up her pace almost to a sprint.

A series of police vans poured across the cobbled open area in front of the Louvre and expelled a small army of french policemen who dispersed into the building. More vans arrived bearing police marksmen; they too dissolved into the Louvre's roofs and high windows. Ordinary gendarmes moved traffic away; re directed cars and asked waiting commercial vehicles to 'move on'. One of these was a brown camper van.

Laura looked up and down the train carriage and noticed how differently the summer commuters were dressed compared to people back home. The french urbanites were more casual yet stylish with the use of hats and colours not normally displayed in an office environment. The train pulled into Gare St. Austerlitz, a memory, Laura reflected, to a distant historic battle. She liked the metro as it took them to the nearby great cathedral of Notre Dame.

"Yeah Dad whatever…….Don't give up the day job…"Mr. Fielding turned around to see the remainder of his family leaving him, clearly thinking that his hunchback performance was embarrassing. A group of Japanese tourists wildly applauded his unexpected piece of street entertainment. The others headed down on towards the impressive edifice that was the Louvre building alongside the banks of the mighty river Seine.

Jacob's eyes widened as the three sided stateliness of the Louvre opened up in front of him. Entering through the Porte des Lions, he could now see the central square, together with its modern glass pyramid visitor centre. "Wow," he gasped.

"Not sure about the length of the queue" said Matthew. Despite this, the queue moved swiftly and they were soon inside the 'pyramid'.

"More X-ray scans Dad!" as they all descended into the main and massive central area. Jacob felt reassured by the vast and milling crowds all crossing, meeting and queuing. Mrs. F. went off for tickets whilst the others joined swarms of people waiting and decided to sit on the smooth marble floor. No less than twenty seconds later, a large man shouted at them from behind. Jacob feared the worst and that the game was up. They all stood quickly and the children's father even held his hands up, only to find a Louvre attendant who, for the hundredth time that morning, was instructing people that sitting on the floor was "interdit" - not permitted, a phrase they were to become familiar with.

"Dad" said Laura "don't draw attention to yourself."

"No, you're right" he said. "Sorry it might have given us away."

"No I don't mean that, it's just embarrassing" she replied.

"Let's go" announced Jacob as Mrs. F returned with the tickets. They set off to view the *Venus De Milo.*

"A fine example of Michelangelo's work" said his father upon arrival at the aforementioned statue. The family bustled in with all the other peoples of the world to get a closer view and a picture.

"Are you sure?" said Jacob, not being overly impressed with the lump of white and armless stone, "it says here that it was probably first century found in Greece, so no one knew who had carved it.".

"Did I say Michelangelo?"bumbled his father.

"Yes. Sure Dad" said Jacob smiling.

"Nathan, come on" said Laura noticing her brother, "Stop wandering off in a dream."

Jacob gazed at the many rooms dripping with well known masterpieces, but there was now only one thing to do. That was to follow the masses who, it seemed, were drawn as if by a magnet to a very solid room several corridors away.Everywherehe looked were tour guides and large numbers of gazing people. He eventually arrived with the others in one of the long and vast exhibition halls. Jacob sensed his destiny just ahead.

"It's just around this corner" he said looking at a map.Turning the corner they were met by a mass of people who were all clamouring to get close to the main attraction. The far wall was actually a huge divider that halved the vast chamber.On this dividing piece of what seemed like a suspended slab of marble, was one small painting, dwarfed by the size of the wall it was hung upon.

"It just seems like a small dark stamp on a large envelope" said Nathan.

"An impressive description, your teacher Mrs D would be pleased!" patronised Laura.

"The Mona Lisa" said Jacob.

Closer and closer they edged, buffeted by the crowds.

"I can't see" called the six year old Matthew, who was instantly lifted by his father. The mesmerizing picture had drawn in and captured the crowd, bringing it further in. No one wanted to depart early, despite pleas from the museum's security attendants, trying to keep a constant flow of visitors around the closest area to the picture.Jacob pressed into get a better look. He could see Matthew sitting on his father's shoulders. He had heard about the lady's eyes which were alleged to follow you where ever you were. To prove this Jacob moved into the middle of the crowd and to both sides, often with much manoeuvring and complaints from those around the busy stage. True enough the eyes always looked straight at him.

The family gathered back at the far end of the hall. They were puzzled.

"But Mum," said Jacob, "how could anyone do this?"His question was interrupted by a pack of policemen who marched in and cleared the way for a group of distinguished looking dignitaries.

"Wow Mum, look, it's our Prime Minister!" said Jacob.

"Look," said Mrs. F "it's the French Premier as well".

A voice in two languages on the P. A. system announced that the special visits of the two premiers coincided with the 'additional security being provided in today's climate of international terrorism'. With this announcement, a huge piece of glass appeared from the ceiling and descended down slowly over the existing wall, eventually covering the Mona Lisa itself. Laura noticed a faint flicker of light around the picture. A round of applause ensued and then all the VIPs departed, quite pleased with themselves.

"Where's Jacob?" asked Mr F..

"Probably somewhere..." replied Laura uninterested.

"There he is right at the front of the crowd" answered Mrs F. She called to him and eventually Jacob was pulled away from the masses who were still clamouring for a close up of the priceless masterpiece.

"I'd been there all the time Mum, it was her eyes, you know La Joconde. It felt like they were drawing me into a trance, I couldn't move".

"Look again, there!" said Laura pointing. "There's another flicker of light across that massive new glass cover over the picture and wall". She turned to her brother and both babbled a mix of frenetic and desperately gobbled messages.Liking order, especially in such a chaotic place, their mother shouted,

"Now one by one please".

"Ok, well, that glass cover covering the Mona Lisa, well I've seen a flicker of light around it twice now" said Laura.

Jacob carried on... "Well the picture, it kept me looking at it but when I got up close it seemed different, not quite as deep, not so rounded somehow, you know less dramatic than I'd seen it in pictures".

"So what you are saying," deduced his father "is that there's a problem here".

"Yes, yes" they both pleaded.

"And that you think something dodgy is going on?"

"Yes, yes" again they answered.

"But you know this thing, it's almost un-stealable?"

"Look, look" shouted Nathanwho normally found everything enjoyable. Not this time, there was an edge of fear in his voice, "It's that man, you know. Him!"

True enough, the grim and dark figure, still wearing his long city coat and black leather gloves was, this time, directing a group of men who had acquired official Louvre uniforms and were opening the side door to the new dividing glass wall behind which the Mona Lisa hung. They moved inside.

"It's just like the headphone stuff we overheard" said Laura.

Jacob couldn't help wondering how bold the robbers had been, especially as the VIPs were all there as well.

"How did they do it Laura?" asked Nathan.

"Oh I think the glass had an image of the picture projected on to it" she replied

"While they were stealing the real one" added Jacob, keen to show his grasp of the crime

"So the tourists are taking photos of a glass projected picture?" asked Matthew.

"C'mon," said Jacob "let's follow them".

"Oh no," said his father "just when I needed a quiet holiday."

The family proceeded to follow the gang whilst the crowd looked on at an electronically faked Mona Lisa amid the chaos of departing dignitaries.

"Look, we mustn't draw attention to ourselves and don't let anyone see we are following them" urged Laura. Whenever any member of the gang turned back the six members of the family quickly examined an old statue or painting, or simply hid.

Suddenly a deafening noise of screaming, sirens and military style crescendos of alarms filled the old museum, causinghysterical shoutingand mass panic in the swarming crowds.

"Sounds like the thieves' cover is blown" shouted Jacob.

The leaving crowds panicked. Almost immediately, the Louvre's security plans snapped into action. Attendants swiftly followed a pre-set health and safety plan, whilst armed guards set off in pursuit to find whoever had committed the robbery. Descending metal shutters closed around every door.

"How will they get out of this?" asked Nathan.

"Shh" replied the others as they hid behind a particularly large conquering 'Horse and General' statue.

"Mum how can they escape?" asked Matthew.

"Yeah and where's that man the leader?" added Nathan.

Amid the chaos, Jacob noticed one of the men roll up a canvas and stuff it into one of the furls of a nearby statue. This piece of white sculpted marble was of a French King and his flowing stone robes made an excellent hiding place.

"Hey!" whispered Jacob "They've put it there!"

"What?" answered Laura.

"Yeah, it's the picture you know the real Mona Lisa thing, it's in there now in that king statue".

Jacob was sure that his assumption about the picture was right and this was confirmed, at least in his eyes; when he saw the thieves take off their outer clothes, throw them in a nearby bin to reveal authentic looking attendant uniforms with fake I. D. cards on chains around their necks. The men dispersed and started commanding the droves of visitors, acting as officials with swiftness and confidence.

"Oh yes"said Nathan, "that's what they were doing at the Fontain-place thing. I recognize them now in their gear". The armed police suddenly arrived. "I don't think they've found any suspects or thieves or even the picture."

"No you're right" shouted Laura "the gang have vanished into thin air".

Quite innocently Matthew asked. "But mum why did he put the treasure in that statue's cloak?" His mother whispered back,

"Because everyone will now be searched on the way out. Then the gang will return some other time when things have calmed down".

"Yes Mum" said Jacob "it's called stashing the goods".

"How do you know about that?" asked his mother. Jacob shrugged, a little embarrassed.

Nathan, though, had an idea.

Chapter Seven

In the thick of it

" *Nous avons une grande urgence*" ....a crackled French voice came from the small hand held radio left discarded on the marble floor.
"What's happening Mum?" shouted Matthew.
"Everyone's trying to find out what's happened, that's why all the security people are shouting and bossing everyone about" his mother replied and then asked a passerby for a translation of the announcements.

"There is an incident majeur ici, oh pardon, here in the Louvre, who knows what?"replied a sympathetic french woman. Gossip, rumours and much shouting now spread like wildfire.

"Well" shouted Laura "what shall we do now? We can't let them get away with it!"

"No" gasped her father "but if we tell the authorities where the painting has been stashed we could be in for some pretty close questioning and I don't fancy that myself!"

"I know," said Nathan, "Let's hide it again so the gang can't find it."

"Brilliant thinking!" said his mother. "In that case we need you to do it as we might arouse suspicion".Her husband went white.

"Yeah over there, slip it rolled up behind that painting of a priest or whatever there," shouted Jacob pointing.

"A cardinal," corrected Laura. "Look, Matt, Jacob, me and Dad, we'll go up to the security people asking questions in English to distract them. Meanwhile Nathan and Mum go to the old king's statue." Everyone followed Laura's plan. Nathan quickly inserted his arm into the marble king's cloak and clutched the soft, old canvas. His mother then pulled him over to the targeted picture.

"Is the decoy plan working Mum?"

"Yes now get on my shoulders quickly."

Nathan concentrated as he inserted the priceless canvas behind the old dusty cardinal. As soon as he'd done this and jumped off his mum's shoulders, he could see that the decoy had worn thin. This was just as well because the entire area had been cleared. The family followed the crowds.

"Everyone's being checked" said Matthew as he watched people spilling out into the massive courtyard where everything was in a state of confusion. Bursting with suppressed excitement and a touch of fear, Jacob found the exit and called the others.

"Look" said Nathan. "It's them again. It's… one of the men, the same one that heard us talking at the other place when we gave the earphones back. He's got a mobile phone".

"Right let's get a taxi back to the station" said his Father. Soon a large taxi was spotted and hailed.

Nathan felt a huge sense of relief. He thought about having touched 'it' the 'priceless picture', the alarms, police, the gang…But now the taxi was a little zone of protection as it zoomed along the Parisian streets, he felt safe for now. He noticed that the traffic was quiet as the taxi slipped into the main road bordering the river Seine.

The excitement of the day and the many hours on foot took its toll on him as the comfortable taxi seats caused his eyelids to drop.

BANG.

A huge jolt hit the vehicle. The taxi spun around, throwing him to the right. His safety belt cut into his chest sharply and the shock was startling. The taxi slewed further to the right, mounted the kerb from a sideways angle and lurched dangerously. For an agonizing few seconds, the vehicle tipped onto its right hand side. Nathan could see the road close by his window as the momentum of the vehicle seemed to balance and then sickeningly topple over onto its side on to the pavement. The taxi slammed into a waste bin which thankfully did not penetrate the doors or side windows but was flattened in the impact.

Pressed on his side, broken glass everywhere, Nathan could hear the surrounding traffic stop and other drivers running over to the overturned taxi as it came to rest on its right hand side. He heard people calling for an ambulance and the police. The few minutes it took for the police to arrive seemed like hours to Nathan. He sensed he heard the squeal of a fast car leaving, but then looked around for the others. He was pressed against the shattered window, now on the ground. Matthew was next to him having slipped out of the upper part of the seat belt leaning hard against him. Laura and Jacob were in the back row, but they were moving.

"Matthew, are you ok?" his mother cried.

"I think so but I'm scared" he replied

"It's ok we'll be out in a minute" Laura added, she hoped.

Nathan's mother checked everyone and thankfully no one was badly hurt, though Nathan spotted that the driver did not move at all. He could hear people running up to the car and climbing onto the taxi. He saw a man signaling through the left hand windows which were now on the top.

"Matthew undo your belt and reach up".

"Stand on me" said Laura who pressed the window button. Nathan could hear that many people were talking to them, all in French.

"Nous sommes anglais," shouted his father, which prompted a change of pace in the number of words coming his way.

"Matthew you go first" said Mrs. F. Matthew climbed up towards the side windows and, with the help of many hands, pulled himself up through the window and onto the top of the taxi. More outstretched hands beckoned him to slide down the roof and towards safety. A large French lady knelt down and put an arm around Matthew. Soon Nathan, then Jacob made a similar journey and joined Matthew, holding each other for comfort. Laura and the parents quickly followed. The six of them now received some attention from the noisy, siren flashing ambulance.

"At least the driver's ok," said Matthew, "I think he needs the hospital doesn't he Mum?"

"Yes Matthew, he does and I think we should just slip away quickly. In the middle of the chaos, they walked away, a little bruised and very confused. Thinking how the taxi was hit, Nathan wondered why no one volunteered to say what he was thinking.

The mood that night was dominated by shock, but at the same time there was just a hint of excitement and amazement in their feverish talk.

Later, collapsed and exhausted in his bed, Nathan was just about awake. He wondered about the day, the mad events at the Louvre. He reached down below his bed and pulled up his bag, put it under his pillow and slept almost immediately.

Unbeknown to all of them, a slip of paper was slowly pushed under the front door of the gite.

Chapter Eight

Of lilies & letters

5th August

Long-legged and stationary, with a long spear-like poised bill, a heron waited and waited. On its one stalk resembling leg it stood, patiently, in the languid current of a small river which flowed slowly round a gentle bend, cornered by an eroded bank. From the bank flew a bullet of red and vivid blue, as a kingfisher accelerated at pace, dived into the river and before the heron could launch its long bill, stole a small young fish which had just come into the heron's vision. Having successfully evaded the taller bird's anger, the kingfisher shot away. The heron waded out of the river, its conquest lost. It stood forlornly on the bank.

On being disturbed by the throttle and grumble of a shiny chrome motorbike, the heron opened its ungainly cumbersome wings and flew away. The motorbike rounded the bend of a small country road which ran parallel to the river.

Breakfast took place in relative silence compared to the jabbering of the night before and it wasn't until Matthew noticed the paper by the door and brought it over, that the tempo picked up.

"What's that?" said his father, "Probably some French double glazing adverts or a holiday home purchase offer." As soon as Matt picked it up, he knew that the note was no advert as it was not printed, but hand written. This could only spell trouble.

"Look it's to us!" said Matthew. This piece of news now stopped every clink and rattle of breakfast spoon and bowl. All eyes were on Matt who eventually slowly read out the message in full as he knew nothing could be kept secret from the family.

To Matthew, Nathan, Jacob, Laura, Mr. and Mrs. Fielding.

You have been remarkably busy for British tourists in this fine city. Your ways of enjoying the holiday do seem to be extremely unusual. I would be most grateful to make your acquaintance and discuss some business with you. Meet me at Giverny on the main bridge in Monet's water lily gardens today at 14:00.

Yours
A friend.

Matt wondered who the friend was. He heard the remainder of his family talking and asking questions.

"Is it a friend or an enemy?".... "Are we being led into a trap?"….. "Who was it?"..... "How did they know where we are staying?"

Matt cut through with his own,

"When was the note pushed under the door?" It all went quiet.

"Well" answered Laura eventually. "Because the note had been delivered while we were asleep and because nothing bad had happened, then it must have come from a friend". She smiled optimistically.

"Funny friend," said Nathan, something that everyone agreed with.

"Well" said Mrs. F. "so much for my plan to amble along the Champs Elysees."

Matthew held onto the note during the silent journey to the small village of Giverny. Here he realised that the paintings and garden of Claude Monet, the grand master, were the main attraction. He saw how big and immaculate the grounds were, yet also wild, an oasis of calm and peace.

"I've always wanted to come here," said Mrs. F.Her voice, though, contained a mixture of excitement and worry, "let's go to the water lilies" and off she went.

Matt walked into the main garden and thought that it was not bad, for a garden. He recognised now the paintings from the kitchen wall back home. He could tell his mother was impressed and even the others weren't complaining. An hour was spent perusing and drifting around the bridges and walkways. It seemed to Matt to be a place which offered some safety. He saw the bridge, the one in the big picture at home and walked onto it.

"Come over here everyone! Let's have a family picture." Overhearing him, an enthusiastic german offered to take a picture with the camera.

"Danke Schon" replied Mr. Fielding in a faded attempt to recapture his 35 year old 'O' level German certificate. Laura lingered savouring the lilies and depths and hues of the different shades of green.

A black leather glove gripped her shoulder and suddenly the peace of the garden disappeared in a cold rush of fear.She swung around with the others to meet her worst fears.

"Bonjour La Famille Fielding, suivez-moi s'il vous plait!" said the voice behind the glove.Laura did not move but was transfixed. In a wave of huge relief, she realised that her would-be archenemy was none other than her hero, 'Mr. Motorbiker'.

The 'friend' raised a single finger to his lips in a warning of silence.

"Quick follow me, you never know who is watching."

With this he took them through an 'interdite' area of the garden to a secluded bench surrounded by an old and huge wisteria which gave them privacy. Everyone settled, on to a solid bench whilst monsieur 'le motorbiker' sat himself on a wooden stool in front of them.

"I should apologise, my name as you've heard before is Ivan, though it is not my real name.Somehow you have stumbled into a major international incident. You witnessed many things yesterday about the whole affair so you now need to follow my instructions very carefully."

Matt just about kept up with his strong French accent.

"Now look here," said his father rather stuffily, "we are very grateful, for what I'm not sure, but I've had enough of this drama and stuff, I just want a quiet holiday."

"Mais c'est impossible" replied Ivan, "you are too involved, you need me now".

"How do you mean need you?" asked Jacob.

"Oh, mais oui mes amis, you do. Somehow a number 48 was placed by deception on the pole to make you go to a fake gite. You were to be trapped and part of the bigger plot."

"What do you mean trapped and bigger plan?"Mr. Fielding asked.

"The Dark Movement, for that is the sinister organization that is behind this activity, has targeted your family to play a role, I guess perhaps to innocently smuggle certain items out of France. Who would suspect an ordinary family like yours?"

"Hang on, we aren't ordinary" blurted out Laura.

"Non, mais oui" accommodated Ivan, "I think I agree now, excusez-moi, mademoiselle" and with that he gave a 'three musketeer' flourishing bow. His reference to the Dark Movement sent a shiver down Nathan's spine, not something he wanted to hear.

"Yes but why us?"he stammered.

"Ah well maybe later, mon ami. What I can tell you is that I've had to get you out of some problems and I think we will still have to work together over the next few days. You have been tracked for many months."

"Yes" said Matthew "I knew I saw something outside the window at Christmas remember Nath?"

"Oh yeah the cars," added Nathan "those two cars and the camper van, they seemed to have crashed and what happened to that man in the boot?"

"What!" shrieked Mrs F. "You saw a body? In our road?!"

"Well yeah I think so."

"Oh my…" Mrs F sat down and breathed deeply.

Ivan continued

"And Nathan I had to help you twice."

"Twice?" said the puzzled boy who looked at his parents for an answer.

"Yes" continued Ivan "do you remember being locked in the toilet at the motorway service station? Despite no-one believing you, you were locked in to try to force your parents to compromise, I unlocked your door, but by then you had become separated."

"Oh", he said, with a warming smile "and what was the other time? Oh yes I know when I got separated on the ferry."

"Yes" said Ivan "the Movement had sent another operator to pull one of you four away, he might have succeeded were it not for me."

"So how do you explain Christmas Eve and the random choice of a blindfolded finger picking out Paris then?" quizzed the cynical Mrs. F.

Ivan deflected the question.

"So, Laura, it wasn't just the Alps that were raised up on the globe then?"

"Oh I know yes," relied Laura excitedly

"So you think they made us come here? Rubbish!" replied her father dismissively.

"No Dad I remember when I went to get the globe there were fingerprints in the dust".

Ivan looked sad. "I must not say but we had interrupted the Movement which was monitoring your activity, one of our staff broke into stop them and protect you but...." he paused for a while.

"Oh yes I had a phone call once and there were some strange clicks too" added Laura. Everyone was quiet and looked at Ivan. He looked up at them with his faraway gaze.

"So mes amis it looks like you have had les visitors who may have, how do you say, shaped your selection somehow?"

"Well I can't believe all that" Mrs F curtly responded.

"Au contraire, Madame, I must emphasize that you, your family, have been set up as part of the Movement's plan to carry out such an audacious act." Ivan concluded with a telling question.

"So who is to believe you and your story? The French authorities? Mais non. The British Embassy? Mais non. Which leaves, ah yes, the international syndicate of crime behind this situation of which you are the only ones who actually know where their treasure is."

"I think we need another family conference", announced Mr. Fielding who quite decisively took the other members of the family to a different bed of roses to discuss the situation.

After ten minutes of frenetic conversation they all marched back to the waiting Frenchman and Mrs F took up the discussion.

"OK we'll trust you, not that the other options seem that inviting, but we think you are OK. There is however one condition…"

"Which is?" replied Ivan.

"That you tell us who you are and why you've been, as it were, helping us."

"Ah very simply, I am working for the French and British Secret Services."

A passerby would have clearly heard six very loud gulps, but as the vicinity had been carefully chosen for privacy, the family's amazement was kept to the hanging wisteria.

"You what?" demanded Laura. "Prove it" she demanded. Ivan thought, long and hard.

"OK" he said, "here's my card. Call me when you believe me", and with that he slipped behind one of the bushes and disappeared.

"Call me when you believe me, what he is on?" said Jacob, though privately, he wanted to believe him.

"Right, well, nice gardens, let's go back to the gite for a cup of tea, some cake and a good old game of Cluedo or even better still, Monopoly and all this stuff will just go away" said Mr. Fielding.

"I don't believe it, we are lost again in this spaghetti motorway system!" shouted their now irritable father who had lost his temper with the challenges of outer Paris at rush hour.

"I might as well rip this up" said Mrs. F. waving the map.

"Look Mum, two police motorbikers" said Jacob.

"You're right, look on both sides; they are waving their white gloves to follow them."

"Oh no what have I done now?" groaned their father.

Despite the huge traffic jam, the police outriders took them via the hard shoulder and onto domestic roads.

"Oh Mum look all the lights are turning green!" shouted Nathan from the back. The car arrived back at the gite in a third of the time it should have taken and with a roar of their engines the riders vanished, not to be seen again.Parked, but not out of the car, the four children pleaded with their parents.

"It must be true now" Jacob said, something his parents had to agree with. His father dutifully took Ivan's card and called him.

After a huge tea, Matthew suggested *Consequences* his favourite game and he explained the rules.

"Right, get a piece of paper, fold into eight sections, first section is a boy's name, then fold it over and hand it to the person on the left. The next section should be filled in with the boy's job.

Then pass it on until the eight sections are completed then the list is read out loud as a story."

"Ok" said his Father, "no references to bottoms, snogging, or 'you loser' please". This was roundly ignored and the stories left them in painful laughter. Later while the boys giggled themselves to bed with several loud and uninhibited bottom noises, Nathan placed his bag under his pillow again.

August 6th

Alone in her bedroom, Laura awoke. The sound of a motorbike and a small noise at the door distracted her sub-conscious just enough to wake her. She wondered about the holiday. It had been like no other and even now felt she was reading a badly written children's story, like her father's, which seemed too wild to believe. She stood up and passed the noisy and rather earthy smelling bedroom where her brothers were all snoring. She paused a minute and thought about the situation they were in. 'Why couldn't they just find a pool and ignore all this stuff?'

She continued wondering and thinking as she descended the wooden curved staircaseto discover a package which had been pushed through the front door, hanging just inside the letter box at an angle. Again it was addressed to the family using each name individually.

Laura quickly picked it up, returned back upstairs and sat on her sleeping father who woke complaining. She told him what she had found and this alerted her brothers who all piled in on top of their parents' bed as though it were a Christmas or birthday celebration. There were many mumbled complaints from their desperate-to-sleep mother.

"Not another one" said Nathan

Inside was a sealed brown manila envelope with a typed message on the front.

Eyes only M, N, J and L & Parents Fielding.

"Ok Laura, open it then" said her father.
"Twelve tickets, six for the Louvre at 11am".
"Not again" said Jacob.
"And the second six tickets say Versailles Palace; these have a handwritten note on each one, this time reading 4pm." She looked up, nodded and noted a silent agreement to get on with the next stage; there was no debate about what to do. She held the tickets firmly, they had determined the day.

Chapter Nine

<u>Paris déjà vu</u>

With her back to Notre Dame Cathedral and gripping the tickets, Laura noticed a brown camper van pulling into a large square where passing traffic came nearest to the Louvre. Its occupant got out; looking at what was clearly a flat tyre. As he begun to remedy the situation, Laura said,

"I'm sure I've seen that van before."A security attendant signalled them to another entrance and pointed to the ticket.

"Porte F", he announced on close inspection of the ticket.

Having passed through the inevitable X-ray machine, the six of them wandered along an empty corridor, on to another empty one and then another one.

'Where is everyone else?' wondered Laura. The railed off route took them to an empty antechamber. As the door, through which they had come, clicked shut, it had a sort of conclusive sound and, on checking, didn't reopen.

"Oh great" said Jacob "what do we do now?"

He investigated the smooth marble walls which offered no handle or exits anywhere.

"Well Hercule Poirot, any bright ideas now?" quizzed Mrs. F.

"Ah well" he responded "I have le cunning plan…"All eyes were on him. Silence ensued. "Well only joking" he continued.

And then a voice sounded, which made them all jump. No loudspeakers were in sight.

"Please sit down" the voice was authoritative and female, rather like Jacob's Headteacher. Once they were all seated, the voice continued.

"Your involvement in this situation is crucial, your attention to my instructions critical and your concentration will be pivotal. Go through the door and try to act like tourists.Nathan, you must retrieve the item from the place where you hid it and place it inside your backpack. Having done this, and without anyone seeing you, you must all proceed carefully and swiftly to the Palace of Versailles. A taxi will take you there, ask for Christian. At that moment instructions will be sent. You must obey all of these commands each one of you, from your father to Matthew. I repeat, your involvement is crucial. You now have five minutes to devise a plan, the door will then open. Be warned, your enemy has now realized that the original location where they placed the item, is now empty. They will be watching and looking for you!"

With this idea circling in their heads, and after a pause in the lecture of ten long seconds, the voice finished with "and thank you, good luck."

Silence prevailed again as they absorbed the words. Nathan held his bag close in a reflex action. Jacob was always up for a challenge and excitement, but he noted that the word 'enemy' had been used. This he did not like but still didn't want to show any fear and was conscious of his older sister. Instead he vented some of his frustrations

"Your involvement is crucial" he said with a mocking copy voice.

"What door? There is no door" said Matthew.

"Look, come on" said Laura, frustrated, "we've only got four and a half minutes. This is what I suggest."

Amazingly, or so it seemed to her father, this twelve year-old girl had devised a plan to retrieve the picture.

"Right we need to setup four decoy actions and a rendezvous in a different exhibition hall. The signal is a large sneeze, then Matthew pretends to fall over near one of the three attendants. Mum looks after him in pretend pain. Nathan and Jacob then play with one of the roped off sections and accidentally topple one of the stands over. Meanwhile Dad, you approach the remaining attendant and ask a meaningless question to distract attention away from the main business.Ok?"

The plan was good and it was such a relief that no one else had to think of one. There was a certain groundswell of family bonding and congratulations given hurriedly to Laura. This she enjoyed, not ostentatiously, but with a degree of self confidence and enjoyed leadership.

Even Jacob put a 'well done' sort of hand on his big sister's shoulder, but not for long, he didn't want to seem to be too encouraging. To the second, an opening appeared from nowhere on a wall covered by an old tapestry. Poking her head round it, Laura whispered,

"Right, one by one, I'll give you a signal to move quickly and merge into the crowd. OK?"

Nathan was very nervous. He realised he had to retrieve the canvas. Last time had been easy due to the heavy crowds.

Laura also grew increasingly nervous, more so than the others. Her stomach gripped in a deep fist of fear. She remembered that door knocker and wondered if it was the symbol of the Dark Order. She knew she must conquer this fear and mentally kicked out against the drowning waters of worry.

Just as all of them merged into the room and moved towards their action stations, a little girl sneezed.Laura knew her plan had started wrongly. Matthew thought it was her, fell over and gave an Oscar-winning display of ambulance-requiring authenticity.His father had also gone into stupid British tourist mode with,

"Now look here my good man" (despite the fact that the attendant was a very large woman) and carried on with, "Now was this Michael Angela really a man or a woman? I mean let's face it anyone with a boy's name and a girl's name must be a bit dodgy don't you think?"

Laura was impressed with her father's performance of sheer stupidity which led to the attendant and Mr Fielding looking at paintings of rather large and naked ladies with bowls of fruit and puppy dogs. Laura decided it was time to sneeze so that Nathan, who had diligently waited for the real signal, instantly rugby tackled the stands taking with him some twenty metres of roped off area in a domino-crushing cascade of noise and destruction. He quickly moved away.

Jacob and Nathan double checked that no remaining attendants were watching and slipped into concentrated action. Jacob provided the two handed step for Nathan's right, sweaty trainer and lifted him up. He rose to the old cardinal's portrait, pushed by his brother to reach and grope behind for the crinkly canvas and pulled it free. For one fleeting moment he held and sensed again the importance of this amazing canvas, but knowing only a few seconds of decoy remained, he slid down onto Jacob who provided a silent crash landing. Together they both crouched alone on the floor and checked the landscape.

"Put it in your back pack Nath" instructed Jacob.

Matthew had proved such an effective performer that a stretcher had been called for by the attendants and his mother, realizing that things had gone a bit too far, tried to put off the on-site first aid team who, it seemed, were bored and had nothing to do. The instant first aiders started strapping Matthew with velcro restraints and a neck brace into the stretcher and radioed for an ambulance.

"Oh I'm sure he will be Ok," his mother smiled politely with gritted teeth. "Il est Ok. Non trop bad or whatever you call it".

'Mum's rubbish at languages' thought Laura whorealized that the plan had gone to seed. Her youngest brother was being carried away to an expectant ambulance, while her father had been taken to a small lecture room on Italian sculpture of the fifteenth century by a very enthusiastic (and strong and sweaty) lady attendant.

Laura beckoned quickly to the other two to come out of hiding and to meet at the rendezvous. This point was the 'baggerie' or where luggage was left. Only Nathan and Jacob arrived, so the three quickly left through the main 'sortie' and out into the massive courtyard.

"What shall we do now?"said Nathan.

"Not too sure" said Jacob.

"Nor me" said Laura.

Laura spotted the ambulance parked nearby the entrance and the long queue of tourists waiting to enter the Palace. She ran up to the ambulance. A silent trickling of sweat passed her eyebrows and her long hair was getting everywhere. She saw her brother, this time not acting, but full of real tears as he was still being carried on a stretcher by French speaking paramedics into an unknown ambulance and with his mother nowhere in sight.

Mrs F, it turned out, was being coerced into signing forms by the other paramedic. Laura could see something was needed, so she climbed into the ambulance's driver's seat, searched and was successful. The siren was deafening. Jumping out the passenger side, Laura ran around to the back to where the paramedics had now left and released her brother. At full pelt they set off back for the entrance.

Laura was confused, the main foyer heaved with tourists, languages bounced off the walls from all continents, photos, laughs, babies crying and large maps all filled the high vaulted room. The crowds were dense and swirled around by occasional tour guides and lost children. She was also lost at this juncture of the hot afternoon.

She needed to track her father down and after ten minutes found the room he was in and ended up dragging him out.

"Oh no" said Jacob.

"What" replied Laura running hard.

"One of those men has seen us." Laura's heart thumped. "What did the voice say again?"

"We must now go in a car to Vercy" said Matthew.

"Versailles" said Jacob

"In a car with someone" said Nathan "what's his name?"

No one could remember anyone except Matthew.

"Christian" he said

"Yes" said his Dad happily and picked him up high in congratulation. "Ok, everyone spread out and find the taxi driver."

They kept going up and down the taxi rank and asked for "Christian". Strangely they had several angry responses.

A low whistle caught their attention. A heavily bearded man grunted "venez" and an old gnarled forefinger bade them towards him. He led them to a battered old Peugeot estate.

"Je suis Christian" was all he grumbled quietly.

The parents looked at each other, shrugged and all got in.

"I know we don't know him but who cares?"said their father.

The journey out of Paris was slow, noisy and hot. 'No air conditioning in this heap of rubbish' thought Jacob. 'Some holiday'. Eventually they arrived at the Palace of Versailles.

•••

Matt noticed that, just like the Louvre and Fontainebleau, the Palace of Versailles opened up to a massive courtyard with a huge three-sided building surrounding it. On the left was a winding human snake of people, layer upon layer of patience, queuing for tickets. On the right was another long line of people who had tickets and were now trying to get through the Palace entrance.

The sun was hot and for those just beginning the process it seemed as if a long wait was in store.

"A good job we have tickets" announced Mrs F.

'This better be good' thought Matthew, 'The queue is the biggest I've ever seen.' He worried that this adventure might be too close for comfort.

Nathan gripped his bag and nervously watched it pass through the X-ray check

The six of them eventually made their way into the palace and reached the café. Mr.Fielding ordered six large iced drinks and suddenly he was quite popular.Drinking in silence they all wondered what would happen next.Laura pulled out the crumpled note from her pocket.

"It just says *'go to Versailles palace'* and *'16:00'*. It is now four fifteen"

"Ah well, maybe the scent has gone weak and no one is bothered anymore!" said her jocular but thinly optimistic father.

"I think not," replied her mother coldlystaring out of the windows. The car that had taken them to the Palace was now parked in the main courtyard and Christian was handcuffed in the rear seat.

"Let's hide in the loos" said Jacob.

And with no better idea, they hid in the toilets for half an hour. Hoping that the coast was now clear, Laura came out and knocked on the door of the men's toilet and out came Nathan, Matthew and Jacob.

Just when Laura thought that things couldn't get worse, she recognised one of the gang, who then noticed her as well and immediately picked up his cell phone. The panic factor had multiplied by ten.

"Boys we need to split up, they are on to us, we'll meet at the er………." Seeing a notice, she said the first thing that came into her mind, "Napoleon's bedroom".

The boys dispersed quickly and Laura knew she needed to get to her parents to warn them.

Laura searched for her father and after a few minutes, saw him from the other side of a lecture room that he had wandered into. She desperately tried to send him a message and having nothing to write with, started to act out a charade across the gathered and seated audience. At first she pretended to have a huge hat on and no right arm (or so she guessed) then mimed being asleep. This started to turn heads. Frustrated she could see her father was trapped as one of LeClaw's men had entered the room. She spotted a fire extinguisher, slowly walked up to it and followed its instructions without looking too obvious. At arm's length she pressed the lever and all chaos let loose as people were sprayed with foam and a white blanket filled the room, giving her father the cover to make a break for the exit.

Meanwhile, Jacob had taken on the responsibility of senior male and guided his brothers to Napoleon's bedroom. This room was full of people, so they jumped behind the enormous curtains that kept the chamber dark and shielded it from the sun's harmful rays. Laura arrived and searched the room for her brothers.

"Psst" She looked round and joined the boys.

Not long afterwards, her mother entered.

"Mum" whispered Matthew, "in here "and she was pulled from behind into the curtains.

Nathan felt the straps of his bag heavy on his back and his heartbeat started to race.

Chapter Ten

<u>**Le Rendezvous**</u>

Looking out of the windows behind the full length, heavy curtains Jacob noticed a brown campervan slowly drive up to a vacant car parking space within the grounds of the Palace, near to an orchard. A robed figure got out and put up an official looking sign on the window of the van. A passing security officer noticed him, went up to the window, chatted to the driver and nodded in approval.

Ropes were linked up, *'fermée'* signs displayed, cafes started to clear up, the X-ray machine switched off and crowds, which at one time queued to get in, now waited to find their cars and begin their slow crawl home. Time had ticked on and attendants in the Palace were moving the last few lingering visitors on in an attempt to close down business for the day.

"Where's Dad?" hissed Jacob. He could sense that everyone hiding behind the large curtains was very nervous. The chamber was oppressive in the heat. The quietness exaggerated the tension of waiting, of hiding.

"Mum, how long do we have to wait?" whispered Matthew.

"Sshh" replied his Mother, "careful of that large pot there, don't kick it over".

A few visitors still looked around the bedroom.

At that moment, Jacob saw his father running into the room andgrabbing one of the headsets in a false show of interest in the early nineteenth century. He wandered around studying the laid out notes, despite several polite encouragements from the frank Versailles personnel to leave. Then he caught a whiff of a familiar sweaty leather trainer, which could only be one of his own sons and sure enough, he spied out the front of a shoe under the curtains. He checked the loitering attendants and just when they weren't looking, hid in one of the enormous fireplaces, standing quietly in its shadows.

Eventually all the visitors left and the attendants went about their end of day business, straightening ropes, notices and final checks before they left.

"Mum, mum" called a desperate Nathan.

"What is it?" came the hushed reply.

"I need the loo".

"Well use that pot there."

And so, probably some 195 years after the great general used it, a young eight year old boy from Wales found the chamber pot with great relief and amusement. This was clinically cut short by a familiar and fearsome sound. Those same boots, which were heard in the first dark gite with the eerie door knocker, now visited them again along the corridor leading into the chamber.

Jacob closed his eyes. 'So here we are,' he thought, 'five of us cowering behind large curtains, one in the dark recesses of an enormous fireplace, and who knew what figure of evil is coming my way?'. The footsteps stopped on hearing noisy cleaners' voices along the corridor, the boots' sounds moved swiftly, it seemed, to one side. The sound of more workers chattering in french walking straight into Napoleon's room seemed to temporarily put off this fearful confrontation. Jacob peeked out. It was indeed three busy ladies going about the final checks and clean-up of the day.Part of their duties involved tidying up the usual 'interdite' signs, the roping off of the great bedroom and the pulling of the great curtains around Napoleon's very own bed.

Jacob urgently pulled his mother's arm for attention. He cupped a hand to her ear and whispered,

"We must move very quickly, I think the infra red rays will come on soon and that bad man is just around the corner".

His mother nodded and silently signed for all of them to take off their shoes, even to her husband who was still hiding deep in the shadows of the fireplace. The cleaning ladies bustled off quickly and as soon as they had disappeared, all six of the hiders tiptoed into the drawn curtains of the master bed, closed them and grabbed each other for security.

No sooner had they done this than Jacob heard the cold booted steps resume their march back towards the chamber from wherever their owner had been hiding. The marching boots made his stomach turn in fear. His whispers were being suppressed by an equally scared mother. The six of them gripped each other in a desperate state. This family knot of bodies, in the darkness of the Napoleonic bed, quivered en-masse as the metal-tipped steps now entered Napoleon's bedroom, arrived at the centre of the walkway and stopped. Jacob pictured in his mind the deathly figure and sensed an evil gaze. Across the room he could almost feel its probing presence. The silence seemed loaded with the inevitability of being found. He felt the searching, scanning across the room, drilling into the curtained bed. He felt his brother Matthew shaking and prayed. There was complete silence.

'Phew!' thought Jacob. The presence was now leaving. The relief was physical, almost as if a huge plunger had been withdrawn and the pressure in the atmosphere let out.

"Has it gone now?" whispered Matthew, as his mother's hand had temporarily slipped off his mouth. Her hand went straight back to his face. Jacob looked across at him in anger. The boots started moving again, this time more vigorously, as Jacob knew they had located their desperate prey.Nathan gripped his backpack closely to his chest.

Jacob saw red beams come on through a slit in the curtain around the four poster bed .The steps stopped abruptly again. Clearly thwarted, Jacob heard the dark unseen figure growl roughly, as if from a lifetime of shouting. A faint sound of grinding metal came and went. Jacob knew this was the gripped fist of hatred. He looked at the others and could tell that they also recognised it. The steps turned and marched away swiftly and reluctantly back through the public area. The family was left in a coiled heap of respite and, as the minutes passed, sobbing was the delayed response.

"Well, I think we are OK thanks to those beams, but we are trapped in" whispered Jacob.

"Well frankly I've no idea what to do next though" sighed his mother. Nor, thought Laura had anyone else.

Nathan took his bag off his back. It always seemed a relief when he did that now, though it wasn't heavy at all. His shoulders felt more comfortable. In the darkness, undoing the bag, he touched the valuable canvas, unfurling it a little. He allowed it to curl again in his hands and did his bag back up.

"Let's just rest a little" said his mother and they all slumped, spread out on the vast bed, gradually falling asleep in sheer tiredness and exhaustion.

His father shook Jacob awake. Sodden with sweat and now shivering in the early morning, he clasped onto his father crying uncontrollably.He'd dreamt wildly, of war horses and a monstrous, scimitar waving, dark general. He'd woken everyone else up, which triggered a delayed unleashing of bottled up desperation in his brothers. Having no idea of what to do, Laura remembering her youth club, decided that a quiet prayer was needed.

Chapter Eleven

Le petit-dejeuner

A bell sounded. Everyone woke suddenly and looked at each other. Was this good or bad? Again it sounded. Again they stared.For the third time the bell rang. A discreet cough this time followed the sound of the chime, one which was obviously right outside the curtains. Another polite "ahem…" came from less than a metre from the end of the bed. Jacob was in no fit state to peek through the curtains and so his father looked around to see if there were any volunteers.

"Oh I'll do it," said Laura in a voice of irritation. She peeled back a little of the heavy curtain, then dropped it swiftly in amazement. "Oh my…." she looked at the others, face and jaws wide open.

The curtains were pulled slowly and ceremoniously apart to reveal a very fat man, who was completely bald and profusely sweating. He was wearing a brown long robe.In a rich and mellow voice he said:

"My name is Father Jenks; my master has called me and my team to be at your service. Sadly we could not get to you until two hours ago or else we would have made you a little more comfortable. Please step forward and enjoy the petit-dejeurner I have provided."

Such was the overwhelming warmth and friendliness of his voice and smile that the family nearly climbed over each other in the rush to breakfast. Everyone looked at each other. Jacob hadn't yet had time to gauge whether he was 'ok' or knew anything about his team, but the thought of breakfast took hold!

"All to your satisfaction I trust?" rounded off the very round FatherJenks as the last crumbs of breakfast were eaten.It was then that Jacob realised this man was OK; he could be trusted. He recognised a faint welsh accent and this reassured him. The man had a presence, a glow or something that made Jacob feel good.

Now while dads should be good listeners to their children, Jacob hankered for a trustworthy person to talk to. Father Jenks' rotund presence was more than just his huge physical girth. Despite a super shiny baldness, well shaven jowl and a few beads of sweat upon this large and kindly face, his most prominent feature was the smile.

"How are you young man?" he inquired. Jacob just shrugged his shoulders in a resigned way. Father Jenks bent down to whisper to his ear.

"Don't worry about dreams my son, silly distractions, you can win the battle."

'How did he know about my dream?' thought Jacob in amazement.

"Good breakfast," said Nathan wiping his mouth with his sleeve.

"Excellent" said Father Jenks, "now I must ask you to come through to the next chamber." He walked up to an ancient sword held in the wall by two tarnished gauntlets, turned one and a door opened from below and beckoned them all in.Father Jenks spoke to them as they sat on a long stone bench in a cool stone room, bereft of any other furniture. A simple castle-like arrow window let in a shaft of sunlight which picked out his face. The light shone strongly and purely, the four children basked in its strength and wholeness.

"We haven't long. Already you have met several of us, which is not ideal. Ivan will continue to help you."

"Help us?" said Laura "We haven't seen him since…….. Oh whenever, anyway he's done nothing since then!"

"Ah" said Mr. Jenks "so the infra red beams were luck?"He smiled one of those all knowing kindly smiles and continued. "Now listen to me carefully. What you have is more than art. It is a link to a much bigger situation. We need you to fulfil your role."

He presented them with six passports and two new credit cards. To Laura he gave a leather pouch with the zip along one side. The family gathered around it quickly. There was one A4 size note typed with a list which resembled a quiz or puzzle. It read;

Father's number (in six digits commonly used)
*Ditto for the other five. Take each first#
then - 186610*

The family pored over this puzzle and when they admitted defeat, looked up and began to ask.

"But Father Jenks what…..."

Their questions were but empty echoes around the stone room.He had quietly slipped away and left them.

"I don't believe it" said Mr Fielding "not another room without any doors I just wanted to have a quiet holiday."

"What's the other thing?" asked Matthew. The others had been so preoccupied with the puzzle that they hadn't noticed the polystyrene box which was about half the size of a shoe box. Having opened it, Nathan found something he and his father had always wanted, a sat-nav!

"Do you put in a postcard or something for a place you are going to?" Nathan asked and received an impatient 'shhh' from the others.

"Ok, not now Nathan" said his father.

"Postcode is what you are after," whispered Laura.

"But why have they given us this then?" he asked, not yet sensing the irritation factor he was causing. "Let's just put the number of where we are going into the machine and it might tell us where to go" said Nathan.

"Nathan, quiet please" replied his annoyed father.

"... oh but.."

"Nathan's got the answer!" Laura shouted "We need to put the number in the sat nav to tell us where to go, the puzzle tells us that number!"

"Oh yes, Sorry Nath".

"Ok, so we need to work out the number and I think that the six numbers are our dates of birth, you know like mine is 270499"

"But we've no pen" said her mother.

"Just as well," said Nathan "it was given in riddle form so no one else would know it and we need to keep it a secret".

"Yes" chipped in Laura "then you take the first number of each of our six figure birth date numbers which is 1 for Jacob, 1 for me, 1 for

Mum, 2 for Dad, 0 for Matthew and 2 for Nathan".

"Each one of us must remember our own first number from our own birthdays", said Nathan. Matthew closed his eyes. "Yes put them in order that's 211120" Nathan quickly summarised.

"Yes" added Laura "take away the number on the sheet 186610."

"24510" said Mrs F, whose mathematical prowess was well known amongst the family. She smiled a self-satisfied smile.

"Well done Mum" said Matthew. This done, the machine was switched on and the prompt about their destination appeared, Laura keyed in 24510.

"What's up Matthew?" asked his Mum. Matthew looked blank. He had been gripping nine of his fingers very tightly.

"Oh it is to remind me of my number".

The exasperation and laughing of the other three children only just missed causing a few tears from Matthew. The number was entered and a clear map of France instantly appeared on the small screen with a route and mileage and all sorts of information. The destination was a tiny village near Bergerac.

"Where's Bergerac?" asked Nathan.

Laura then answered by fiddling with the sat-nav controls.

"OK, it's in the south about four hundred miles away."

The family's spirits suddenly sunk again with the prospect of a huge journey further away from Britain. The sat-nav screen suddenly flashed up and spoke out the following.

"You must proceed with your journey now."

The emphasis on that "now" was very direct. Another previously non-existent stone door ground open, leading them back into the busy reception area.

"Well shall we stay or continue to be involved?" asked Laura.

"If we don't stay," said her father "the rolled up item could be dropped off at a gendarmerie and we could disappear into the crowds."

"But we must continue" said Jacob and soon all the children joined in, "…and we want to go to the south of France".

"It's too far away" said their Father. Just then one of the airplanes from nearby Orly Airport came in to land and so did an idea from Nathan.

"We could fly there".

"Oh and I've got a shedful of money" said his annoyed father.

"But you have, that man Father Jenks gave you two credit cards".

This pulled his father's rejection right from under him and for a moment he was speechless.

Mrs F looked sideways at her husband in one of those 'well maybe he's got a point' sort of ways, which then set off more pleading from all the four children. Mr Fielding had no defence left. He gave in, "Let's find a taxi".

"Er dad," said Nathan "you know your idea about not getting involved? Well look over there".

Just fifteen cars away from them, were two of LeClaw's men working their way from car to car, desperately looking, desperately searching.

Chapter Twelve

<u>Sanctuary</u>

 Sunflowers stood to attention. Rows and rows and rows looked up at their brilliant master in the sky. A winged shadow temporarily passed over them as a large passenger jet landed in the shimmering heat haze on the runway of Bergerac Airport. It almost gasped from its flight into the southern french heat. An array of various vehicles swarmed around the plane in order to empty its luggage, occupants and refuel. Cleaners boarded and swept through.

Laura listened to the conversation her father was having in the taxi at Bergerac airport. "Oh Laura, can you give directions?"

"No problem" announced Laura, "I'll use the sat-nav".

The taxi driver needed some persuasion, however Laura's father presented him with a flourish of euro notes which did the trick, much to his wife's annoyance.

Laura gave the directions in her debutante French. Several "a gauche" and "adroit" commands were successfully given and after about twenty minutes they found themselves on a tiny country lane. She noticed the scenery passing by.

The road was squeezed in between maize cornfields which stood tightly packed with strict agricultural efficiency. Laura noticed how some fields of sunflowers were more advanced, older and looked sad with drooped, heavy seed heads still trying to point toward the sun. All the sunflowers seemed slightly scary to her as if each one was in some robotic way, obeying the sun never to step out of line unless their days were over.

"A gauche" directed Laura.

This, as it turned out to be, was the final command for the taxi driver. His car slowly turned off the tarmac onto a white stony bumpy track which led between towering conifers. The rest of the hot landscape was deciduous, broadleaf tree copses, so the presence of these conifers gave the driveway some sort of distinction. Descending a very steep section, the taxi pulled into a small car park which was outlined by a large and ancient pagoda with an old grapevine draped around it.

As Laura got out, a vivid green parrot squawked and took off with a flash of its slender, red tipped wings. The bursting into life of a water sprinkler had sent this luminescent bird away to find a quieter corner of the garden. A showery fine mist now hung over a lush herbaceous border which glistened with its new found evening dew. Flowers of all shades, awoken from their siesta, opened banks of perfume and a heady scent drifted luxuriously around the well kept gardens.

A green square of lawn was surrounded by old and rustic renovated farmhouse buildings on all sides. Barn and grange conversions and what turned out to be a pigeon house adaptation, stood on three of the sides, while an impressive manor house completed the square. All four buildings were roofed with red terracotta and slightly misshapen tiles. The complex was surrounded by meadows which sloped down to a river valley and tiny village. Behind the main house there stood a quite outstandingly tall and large tree amid other large trees. Jacob noticed this special tree as he craned his neck upwards.

Any concerns as to where to go were answered by the sound of a very old tractor chugging along in a field. It turned off to the left and came straight towards them. The driver pulled up alongside, switched off the cylinder mowers and dusted down loose grass clippings from his old leather gloves. He took off his dark sunglasses and wide white hat to reveal a tanned, yet friendly face.

"Welcome, welcome, so good to see you, my name is Peter". All their minds were put to rest by his presence. "Now you must be the Fieldings?"

"Yes we are" exclaimed Matthew.

With spread out arms and hands open to them Peter exclaimed,

"Everything is all right here, don't worry Father Jenks called me."

It appeared to Laura that Mr Jenks had arranged everything.

Just then, a lady in wellies, a wide brimmed hat and an armful of honeysuckle flowers from a separate walled garden, joined them. The flowers filled the late afternoon air with a scent so sweet that one needed a few seconds to take it all in.

"Hello I'm Nancy".

She was quite short and with a head of long jet black shiny hair.

"We are here to really look after you" and she put up an arm with an index finger pointing at them in instruction, "... and we know the whole story so no need to tell us anything, we've been put in the picture".

"Picture aha" responded Peter with a huge belly laugh. "Good one yes picture ha, ha".

Nathan gripped his bag tightly as if the secret was out. But sensing this Peter looked at him and said;

"Don't worry Nathan;" though no introductions had been made "it's all okay here."Then looking at all of them, he continue, "Now please come with me and just enjoy."

He and Nancy led them to one of the converted barns and showed them to their new holiday home. Entering through the lounge, they looked up and saw a three sided landing, almost like a minstrel's gallery, all in an old oak and stone finish. The kitchen was open, wide and seemed to have everything in it. The fridge was bursting with fresh local food and there was a huge bowl of almost limitless varieties of fresh local fruits set in the middle of a large oak kitchen table. The children wandered around asking questions.

"What's this Peter?" asked Nathan looking up to a large and very old cutting tool fixed high up onto the internal whitewashed wall.

"Ah, well in the old days before tractors and machines, people had to cut meadows and cornfields by hand and this is what is called a scythe. The farmers and workers used to swing it around like this to cut the fields."

"That must have been hard work," Nathan mused as he continued to look up, imagining the farmer cutting the fields in the hot French sun. He pondered over its smooth curving blade set into a stout oak handle.

"For you yes but not for my strength and special powers!" replied Jacob as he flexed his muscles.

"Strength of an ant that's feeling sick I think" added Laura unimpressed with her brother's posturing.

Having showed them everything, their hosts announced,

"Now we will leave you to get settled. Please do use the pool." Peter turned to leave them, but then hesitated and added "Oh, nearly forgot, at 5.30 Nancy and I are having a barbecue for all our guests under the grapevine. Don't bring anything except for an empty plate and a glass."

And with that they waved and left them. Mrs. F. burst into tears. All the tensions of the previous days, it seemed, were all let out into this sanctuary.

Refreshed and exhausted from playing in the pool, having splashed and 'dumped' their father to their hearts content, the children lazed in the water. Matthew asked

"Is it time for the barbecue? I'm starving".

All the other guests had assembled under the eaves of the tendrilled vined pergola, where a fierce, smoking barbecue grill was doing its best to emit taste bud teasing aromas of what turned out to be the thickest, meatiest, tastiest burgers, sausages [which were nearly a foot long], chicken thighs basted in a sweet sauce and lamb chops. Bowls on the long table heaved with salads, breads of all sizes, dips, sauces, coleslaws, and every drink possible was also on hand. Relaxed into their new abode and aided by the plentiful food and drink, the family warmed to all the guests as conversations began and the evening flowed splendidly.

"…..and then", said Nathan, "we saw someone stealing a painting…"
Suddenly the barbecue burst into a small explosion of steam and hissing. Evidently, a large jug of water had been knocked on to it (Laura was sure only seconds before Peter had been using it to pour drinks) and had caused the noisy display. As though prompted by this, Peter offered everyone a large plate of chunky chocolates. In doing this, he bent down slightly and in a secretive hushed tone, warned Nathan ….

"Be careful what you say". Then with his public face to everyone else…. "Well please all charge your glasses and let's settle on the lawn as tonight we are to see shooting stars!"

This caused much excitement to young and old as they stood and stumbled out of their seats. The ever resourceful Nancy stepped out of a shed brimming with rugs of all colours and sizes. The evening had moved on and it was quite dark. Peter brought out a few lanterns, placing each one around the lawn. Eventually most of the guests found their way onto the rugs and sighs of tiredness were followed by exclamations about the glittering stars that were adorning the velvet black sky that night.

"Look at that" said Jacob "that's Leo and there is the Plough."

"No it's not" retorted Laura "the Plough's over there," pointing to the other side of the sky and who knows how many millions of light years away.

The discussions about constellations were interrupted by gasps and shouts as a shooting star burst from the lower left onto the center of the sky.

"Look at that, there, that was great" said Nathan.

"Oh but I didn't see it mum" said Matthew full of tiredness and started whimper. He was cut short by a fantastic array of shooting stars that appeared again in the same corner of the sky. For half an hour shooting star after star appeared from all parts of the sky. Each time someone would predict from where the next one would come and nearly always they would be wrong, which caused much laughter.

Finally Laura carried the sleeping Matthew back to the house to bed. Nathan's bag was still on his shoulders as he lay on his bed. Finally, all found pillows and dreamed of stars, rockets and best of all, nothing.

8 August.

"Mum, look another note" said Nathan who had just got up and broke the quietness of the house. An unease was felt. The note had been slipped under the door like before.

"It's about a trip we are doing today"

"Well read it then," said Jacob who had drifted in.

To the Fieldings.

Tom will be taking you to the Dordogne river for canoeing this morning. Please be ready at 10:00 for collection.
PS oh and bring your bread too, you'll find it where we had the BBQ.
PPS look in the fridge and bring the ham, orange juice,

> *crisps and fruit.*
> *PPPS you'll find the cool bag next to it.*
> *PPPPS on no account contact anyone other than those in*
> *this safe haven.*
> *PPPPPS meeting tonight after dinner at 20:00. The tower.*
> *P and N*

Jacob looked out of the hall window, up at the huge tree and wondered why it drew his attention.

Chapter Thirteen

<u>The River Dordogne</u>

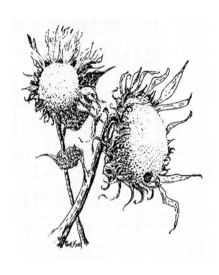

A tall, handsome young man placed blotting pads carefully around a beautifully inlaid round table. At each pad he placed a tumbler and in the middle of the table two large empty jugs. He checked a nearby small fridge, ensured that the table was polished to perfection, carefully positioned a set of high backed leather bound chairs and having finished these tasks he straightened his back and looked out to the magnificent view across the valley, from his lofty and leafy vantage point.

A mud spattered Landover, fresh from an all terrain trip, slowly eased out of an old barn whose roof tapered to a pleasantly angled point. Many vines grew over this garage and tendrils weaved all around its many eaves. Out of the barn, the Landrover chugged slowly with several canoes strapped to its roof.

At 10am the sound of this large diesel engine and a very confident knock at the door bade the family to their canoeing trip. Laura opened the door to let in a handsome young man who she thought was about twenty or so. He stood with a straight back, shoulders pressed back and no one would have been surprised if he had saluted them. Blond hair, slightly tanned face and casual yet ready for action attire, caused Laura to stare just a fraction longer than required before concluding.

"Oh you must be Tom?"

"Indeed I am. At your service."

Laura could have sworn that his ankles twitched a little as if they had been straining to stamp their feet announcing himself as the sergeant to his major.

"Oh this, er well, these are my brothers, Jake, Nathan and Matt and here's Mum and Dad."

"Nice to meet you all, er Mr. Gorvy thought a nice day relaxing on the river would be a good tonic for you, well considering everything else, so well if you are ready, we will go. Here I'll take that".

Picking up the cool bag and swinging open all the doors on his long wheelbase Landrover, Tom jumped aboard and then roared the diesel engine into life.

Laura looked out at the tall corn-plants, sunflowers, harvested hay and verdant vegetable cropped fields. The warmth and drone of the diesel engine was relaxing. Her eyelids sank into a hazy slowness as they met the rhythm and purr of the engine. This was disrupted by Tom shouting.

"Hold on to the handrails".

The rural journey of peace was bumped into a roller-coaster ride as the land rover veered off the tarmac and straight through a harvested straw field, down the tip of another bank and just in time Tom shouted;

"Hold really tight" as the whole vehicle soared almost vertically up a steep bank causing shrieks from everyone. Then just as swiftly, the car plummeted nose down the other side, they just held on.

"And now for the big one" shouted Tom who was clearly relishing the huge sense of weightlessness as the landrover took off from a ramped bank and then landed straight in the river which rose up nearly to the windows. Untroubled by this crazy journey, the landrover turned semi submarine and lumbered along the river bed. Dripping wet, it remounted the other riverbank and drew to a welcome halt on the sand bank of the river bend.

"Hope you enjoyed the journey" Tom announced laughing as his travellers almost fell out of the mud spattered vehicle. Springing up to the roof rack like a bounding monkey, he started to un-strap the kayaks and Canadian canoes and enrolled everyone's help handle the boats down.

Laura, Jacob and Nathan wobbled into their individual kayaks. Nathan fell in to the river getting soaked, whilst Jacob raced off downstream until Mrs F rebuked him. The parents and Matthew clambered into the Canadian canoe and finally Tom followed. His swift and precise paddling was marked in comparison to the Fielding's.

Fish swam in the clear flowing water beneath them amongst the lazy river grasses which swayed in the currents like the green hair braids of a water nymph princess. The ease of paddling, gliding through the clear water, the sense of independence and smoothness of the boats elated all the canoe debutants. The river wound alongside many fields interspersed with high cream and red rock cliffs out of which, châteaux and monasteries appeared to grow organically. All this was the essence of the great and wide river Dordogne, which was refreshing in the growing heat. Sunflowers, corn, tobacco and more sunflowers crowded right up to the banks on either side. Occasionally slightly steeper sections of the river caused a stir of excitement of white-water causing the pace to accelerate slightly from the pedestrian or 'glacial' as Tom was often to describe their rate of progress.

Laura ploughed her kayak into a sand bank in mid stream. The other boats followed her lead. 'Yes' she thought 'this is a perfect place for a picnic'. Gradually each one of the party either laid back in rest or stripped off for a refreshing dip.

The three boys swam and splashed, chasing fish with abandon.Mrs F eased herself onto a comfortable tussock of grass that bordered one end of the sandbank. She closed her eyes and relished the sounds of her family enjoying themselves. Her husband swam across the river in a lazy floating style. Laura sat next to Tom, deep in conversation.

To Laura, Tom seemed quite together and caring.She talked about France, her first impressions and found out how he'd been there for six months. Their discussion seemed to flow smoothly, like the languid river. Large dragonflies flew low sorties over the surface, full of vivid colour. Laura drank all these pictures in, as time floated and passed effortlessly.

"So how old are you then?" asked Laura boldly.

"Twenty" replied Tom

"And why are you here?" Laura continued

"Why am I here? Good question," Tom smiled a worldly tired smile, threw a stone into the river and turned to Laura. "Well I can't say why completely, but I needed to get away from things and then this opportunity arose and I took it."

"Can I ask what you were getting away from?" asked Laura.

"Oh well, my parents died, rather suddenly" he turned and looked down at his feet and the river "and so I needed to" he paused, "to do something."

"Like what?" asked Laura.

"Oh well, these people, you know, who brought you to the Dordogne, I'm working for them" he replied

"Oh the Panel" Laura concluded. For a short moment they were quite still, yet thoughts continued, they smiled, concluding things at that point.

Mr. Fielding began to speak into his mobile cell phone. Tom lurched across and grabbed the phone.

"What did you…?"

"That may give away our position and safety!" shouted Tom. He ordered everyone to swim away. "I'll have to throw that into the river, now!"

"What? Into the river?" exclaimed Mr. Fielding.

"Yes, our lives depend on it" Tom replied urgently, his directions were now orders. "Everyone wade or swim as fast as you can to that copse of trees and keep low in the bushes."

Jacob laughed and said

"Hey Tom this is cool!" but his smile was wiped by Tom's shouts.

"And it may become explosive if you don't do it now."

They all tumbled into the river and strained against the current, verbally beaten on by Tom, who bashed out orders as he strapped the Canadian canoe, Kayaks, life jackets and helmets together, placed the mobile phone in one, pressed last number redial and pushed the boats and paddles downstream with all his might. He swam energetically but expertly, thrashing through the river, still somehow able to shout warnings to the others. He staggered on to the bank dripping and gasping for air before diving alongside the others, cupping Nathan's inquisitive mouth with one hand to enforce the silence.

Everyone waited for the impact of the cell phone, several minutes passed and just when impatience set in, Nathan gasped in horror. The deafening drone of a sleek, black Apache helicopter surged down the river valley, splattering river water to all parts. It unleashed a diver who investigated the tied up boats. He waved a negative arms crossed signal and then was winched back up. On leaving, the helicopter launched a small but perfectly aimed rocket. Within a fraction of a second the rocket hit its target and sent a shower of river spray to all parts denting the riverbed in the process. The canoes and contents were obliterated and strewn everywhere. The menacing helicopter, somehow satisfied, veered off over the hiding escapees whose eardrums rung for minutes from the sound of the assault. Nathan noticed the others clinging onto his parents. He looked intently, showing no emotion and stated "That was meant for us wasn't it?"

Tom called from a walkie talkie on his belt. "Manoir, manoir, request immediate retrieval. Repeat immediate retrieval."

As soon as he had finished his short message he switched off the radio and unplugged the battery. "We must stay absolutely still."

Chapter Fourteen

<u>The tower</u>

Two brightly feathered jays sat on an old strut that once held a sign for the Manoir house. Suddenly, both necks turned right and in a flash of pink and salmon coloured wings, flew off as a very old but superbly maintained Silver Shadow Rolls-Royce, arrived silently in the small courtyard. Two minutes later, nearly as quietly, a small and smoothly shaped Bentley sports car parked on the other side of the courtyard, quickly followed by a silver Aston Martin DBS.

The Landover drew to a halt back at the safe Manoir house complex of eighteenth century farm buildings.

"Can we stay by the pool this afternoon?" asked Matthew.

"I'm doing nothing else" shouted Laura as she jogged away with her towel.

The church bell chimed seven.

On the decked patio surrounded by crumbling walls and overgrown honeysuckle, tea was eaten quietly.

"So where's the tower then?" inquired Nathan.

"What do you mean tower?" asked Matthew.

"You know the one in the note we had today" replied Nathan.

"Er well, I guess it's that tree there" said Jacob. Laura added,

"Well as it is the biggest thing going and there are no actual towers anywhere to be seen…."

Dinner finished, they assembled in the courtyard at ten to eight. The gleaming Rolls Royce silver shadow and bullet shaped Bentley sports car together with the Aston Martin caused a stir with the Four.

"We have company it seems "stated Laura and they all went to the base of the mighty tree behind the large Manoir house in the woods. The tree's bole was vast and its external roots the size of usual large tree trunks.The tree, together with accompanying forest, fringed the edge of one of the many cliffs that defined the great Dordogne River. Its roots grasped into the solid rock of the cliff face and over the centuries, its trunk had soared majestically above its neighbouring trees.

"I think" said Jacob "that we are stumped as to what to do next" he laughed at his own pun only to provoke a scowl from Laura and encouraging clap on the back from his father, a collector of appallingly unfunny jokes.

"Yes Jacob, puntastic! Welcome to the world of the comedian's tumble-weed"

Peter appeared from the other side of the quad wiping his hands.

"Been having to service the tractor today" he explained rubbing grease onto the cloth. "Right then" and with a quick 360 degree visual scan, he grabbed one of the knarled knots that lumpily marked the tree's exterior and held it there for a good few seconds.

"Good" he said "it will be with you very soon" and continued back to the other side of the quad. With a splitting, fibrous noise, a part of the tree's base shifted outwards. This amazed Laura who then stepped inside the enormous towering tree not sure of what was next. A long climb up a spiral staircase led them to a wooden door. Laura opened it and gasped.

"What is it dear" asked her worried mother who by now was permanently on edge. Laura entered a wide, round room, with waxed oak floorboards. In the centre stood a circular polished wooden table, surrounded by high backed leather bound chairs. Laura's gasp was a result of the view which opened up across the river valley, woods and fields and onto the horizon. Simple wooden posts held up a framework of living branches with leaves which rustled softly in the cooling evening breeze. She noticed a large eagle which swooped down to a neighbouring tree and fed its three young in an eyrie.

"Welcome!" announced a deep, deep voice.

At the head of the table, if one can have a head of a round table, sat a very old man. Though old, his eyes gleamed brightly. He was dressed in a cream linen suit, a dark tie and smoked a very large drooping pipe. Puffs of pipe smoke wafted up as if he was drawing on something for the next word. Next to him sat a smiling and rather large man, a serenely beautiful lady and a handsome but serious man.

"Please" he beckoned them with arms outstretched wide. "Please sit".

From outside the room, on a balcony which circumnavigated the whole tree house came the beautiful sound of an acoustic guitar. Its mellow strummings were a fusion of deep classical Spanish with the softness of a rural melody. The gentle notes soothed Laura's nervousness.

"I hope you like our Tower of meeting. We know you've had a.." he hesitated "...challenging time," and drew another intake from his pipe.

"You could say that" chirped in Jacob and everyone laughed.

"Oh but do forgive me I haven't introduced myself and the Panel."

"Mum, is a Panel a wood thing?" asked Matthew. The tension from meeting strangers in an unusual place was lifted.

"It certainly is Matthew, but is it also my name for some special people" responded the old man who placed his pipe in an old bronze holder.

"I am Gorvy, here on my right is Dan Jembos" his right arm opened to a forty-something, who appeared confident and athletic. Matt noticed a scar on his forehead and only one hand resting on the polished table.

"Hi" he responded. It was a brief word, but with a smile which took each and every one of them along with him.

"And here is Kim D'Omest"

Laughing with the confidence of someone used to meeting lots of people, Kim greeted them all by name, giving bigger waves as the children became smaller.

"Good" continued Gorvy "and finally here is Lord Gruntfuttock.". He said this with some grand conclusiveness in his voice, possibly because this rounded off the team. Jacob struggled not to laugh.

"Oh please, it's Grunters, do spare the title" said Lord Gruntfuttock.

Jacob had immediately linked the cars to each one of the Panel members.

"Nice limo Grunters" sparked up Jacob, which again provoked bursts of laughter. "Can I have a ride in your Aston Martin Dan sometime? He continued.

"And what's wrong with mine?" asked Kim.

"Oh, er saving that for a trip to the restaurant" cheekily replied Jacob.

His mother, aghast at his nerve, apologised to Kim but no one heard her through the roars of laughter.

Gorvy raised a finger and a waiter appeared and served each person with what turned out to be a favourite drink of theirs. Laura had to scold the boys both for their slurping sounds and trying to down the drinks in one.

"Oops" said Nathan as all eyes had rested on his drinking achievement.

"Well done my boy, well done"
congratulated the headmasterly Gorvy.

"Yes thank you Tom, no doubt we'll need some more later". Laura hadn't noticed Tom who been pouring drinks.

"And now to business, I guess you must be wondering quite what on earth has been happening to you on your little holiday? Having embarked for a two week trip to France to take in the sights, I guess you have struggled to sit back and relax a little?" The original intention of the holiday had come back to them like a forgotten thought. He continued:

"A difficulty with locating your gite, some strange goings on at the gallery, coming home with more than you bargained for, meeting some disreputable people and staying overnight in unique places. Not to mention a few travel difficulties along the way!"

Nathan whispered to his Dad

"Dad does he know everything we've done?"

"Pretty much I think Nathan" responded the sharp eared Gorvy.

"Even when I forgot to wear my pants to that….."

"Ok Nathan maybe not everything" his father quickly interjected.

"Oh yeah" said Jacob "and I didn't change my pants for five days at the school venture camp!" he beamed with pride.

"Too much information" his mother sharply concluded this line of discussion. Even Dan struggled to hide a faint smile.

"We are very grateful for your hospitality and pleased I'm sure to meet you all….." his father hesitated. He was not sure how to continue especially as all eyes were on him. "But what the hell have we got to do with all this?"

Mrs F looked across at this outburst from her husband.

"Ah yes" responded Gorvy, "Please listen to what I am about to say. You may find it incredible perhaps. Your visit to France was no accident, it was contrived. Ivan has told you of this and of the Dark Movement. You are on holiday; forgive me if I describe it as an ordinary, but splendid British family holiday. Unfortunately you have walked into, or should I say, been guided into, a very large and complex situation. Certain developments have occurred that not even we could have foretold. We are very impressed with you".

Quietness ensued around the table. The suave Jembos at Gorvy's left continued,

"Nice hiding game Nathan" interrupted Dan with a knowing smile. "We have needed to give you some assistance along the way, hence you connecting with Ivan and Father Jenks.".

"And the police bikes?" chirped in Matthew "they were cool". He added with a big smile.

"And the bikes, yes Matthew" responded Gorvy, this time re-lighting his pipe and altering his position in his seat, staring out across the tree canopy. All of which signalled a story to be told.

"So our selection of France was down to you was it?" enquired Laura who could not work this out.

"Oh no, no, no" quickly responded Gorvy, "However we were aware of unnecessary interest in your family from the Dark Movement and later, your plans to come to France."

"Oh", said Nathan, "was that the camper van and the cars chasing at Christmas?" his eyes lit up. "Oh you!" he looked at Dan, "the silver car, was that you?"

Dan nodded.

"What the brown camper van? Were you keeping watch?" asked Laura.

Dan spoke at last "No the Dark movement was tracking you, we tried to intercept it, but one of our operators was taken out by their leader".

"In the black Mercedes?" asked Nathan.

Gorvy continued, "Yes quite right. Anyway my, or should I say our, Panel has for sometime been interested in correcting major wrongs in the world. When we discover that persons or organisations are carrying out dreadful practices, we endeavour to correct them. The Panel here has been richly blessed in this life materially and wish to do something worthwhile. We are all of one accord in that some bad apples require unconventional removal".

The look of surprise from Gorvy's listeners caused him to pick up the tempo.

"Oh don't worry, we don't do anything hugely unlawful ourselves, but the end does rather justify the means you know".

Matthew whispered to his mum "Does that mean they are goodies?"

"I think so" she whispered. Laura wasn't yet quite sure.

"We were working on a project" he emphasized this word "and discovered late in the day that you were the 'mark' or should I say Matthew, the baddies means of removing something very important. I think we all know what that is, don't we Nathan?"

Nathan instinctively held his bag more tightly.

"The only problems for them were that firstly, we found out and secondly, you became quite resourceful."

"But how were we to be smugglers for something that happened by accident?" asked

Laura who was starting to see a little picture emerging.

"Ah yes, accident is a good word because that gang didn't anticipate you evading them at the gite, nor becoming involved in the Louvre as you did. You were always going to be involved, by being coerced into couriering its most priceless treasure out of France".

"But we wouldn't have agreed" retorted their angry father.

"Oh yes you would have, you would have had to!" responded the calm but deadly serious Gorvy. You have a lot of collateral".

"Collateral?"

"Oh but of course" replied Gorvy "you have, after all four lovely, but let's not deny it useful, assets in your children, which they would have used."

Gorvy's attempts at being discrete were immediately understood even by Nathan, who then told Matthew.

"Your selection of France and ultimately of the Louvre are achievements of this Dark Movement. You will recall Laura the interfering of the globe and its raised section over France."

"What?" said Mrs. F"Is that why the globe stopped over Paris?" She looked at Gorvy and then Laura who both nodded.

"Their plans went very wrong and now they are very angry indeed." Gorvy clasped his pipe in his teeth. It seemed to Laura that his pipe helped him pull out more thoughts. He drew in more heady wafts in contemplation. "Yes. Very angry."

"And <u>they</u> are?" enquired Laura.

"Ah a complex story young lady," Laura disliked the 'young lady' reference and its patronizing tone. "Which I will tell you now". Laura watched the old man's long fingers grip his pipe and then stroke his chin in what seemed to be an attempt to muster up his mental energies. Laura reckoned that what could have been a very, very long story was being reduced into something reasonably short and understandable, for most of them at least.

"Our Panel, Order, executive, call it what you will, were alerted a long time ago of a fall out within the French secret services. Such things happen from time to time, however in this case, the aggrieved person became very angry and decided to seek retribution. He was a brilliant operator and had achieved many distinctions in the field, but something happened, we know not what, which caused a rift so great that he, shall we say, 'moved on'".

Gorvy hesitated at this point. Laura could see something in his eyes that said he needed to select his words very carefully.

"This man grew up in Britain and had a break up with his own family." Laura noticed her father, whose gaze had been upon the eagle and its fledglings, looked quickly and intently at Gorvy. The storyteller continued.

"He had not though moved on mentally or emotionally and sought various low level attempts at retaliation. These were traced back to him and he was warned most severely. The then Head of the French Secret Service was uncompromising and brutal".

"Why?" asked Nathan with a boyish interest. "I'm sorry Mrs. F." Gorvy continued gravely "but I must say why. He was a person proven to have stolen, beaten up and, I'm afraid, killed. He caused a great deal of upset," Gorvy hesitated before he disclosed the next statement. "His right hand was removed."

The bold and stark statement left everyone in the room not just stunned but morbidly eager for more information. Gorvy continued.

"He then went to ground. Neither a sighting was made nor was a sound heard from him. Despite the severing of his hand, the punishment did not work. Little did the authorities know that this turned him into a time bomb and turned what values or morals he had left, stone cold. His silence and disappearance were the early signs of his plotting for revenge and retribution."

"Er" interrupted the children's father, "you seem to know an awful lot, here, how do you know it?"

Gorvy again hesitated and looked at his fellow Panel members. Laura discerned the faintest of sideways movement in Dan Jembos' head almost as if he were trying to warn Gorvy of something. Gorvy's eyes looked down at the table as he continued.

"Well let's just say I, or some of us, were in the 'business' so to speak, at the time. Oh I should add that no such butchery was our trademark, I can assure you."

"I should hope not!" added Mrs. F. Laura wondered where this story was going and what her parents were thinking about its levels of brutality for the ears of young children. Gorvy smiled in appeasement. Clearly Laura's question was not going to be fully answered.

"Early signs of unpredictable criminal behaviour were tracked but bore no clues or leads or local information to help. Completely nothing. For example, most crimes in the end are caused by something, yet these random acts seemed to float in a sea of unexplained facts. These crimes were squeaky clean. To all intents and purposes it seemed that a new operator was on the scene, but one who was nameless, without trace. This continued until these events began to develop a loose pattern. Some of the victims, who survived, reported one of their assailants being in possession of a metal and gloved hand, a hand of great strength and power."

Laura looked around at the others; everyone clearly had the same idea.

"Whilst not a trademark, the pattern was clear. It was just by chance that a retired French secret service operative put two and two together and mentioned this to his previous employers. It then seemed a direct link between our man and this mysterious character. The Sûreté nicknamed him 'LeClaw' and that's what we now call him. Of course all this happened a long time ago… Well I think we need a break".

Laura strolled around the encircling balcony and wondered where the meeting was going and what the family's reaction might be. She looked out pensively at the Dordogne panorama. After a few minutes everyone resumed their places at the table. Gorvy continued his tale.

"You have obviously realised that the criminal you have come across is LeClaw. He will stop at nothing to retrieve what you have and to carry on with his plan." Gorvy raised his hands at the stuttering questions. "No, we do not know to what end his plans are leading. I fear though for what end result his festering mind has stored up. Your involvement is imperative. You are the solution to the problem. Whilst we do not know exactly what, there is a special hook you have with Le Claw, which means you are committed".

"So" said Jacob "you know him?"

Again Gorvy hesitated, but Dan concluded.

"Yes we did know him, once". He looked sad.

"But why us?" asked Laura. Gorvy looked at Kim, Dan and Gruntfuttock who all nodded in silence.

"Well" continued Gorvy, "LeClaw is related to you". Laura was stunned. The silence was overwhelming. "More especially, he is your great uncle Mr. Fielding".

Quietness again settled, faintly disturbed by the soft rustle of leaves within the high canopy. Laura looked across to the eyrie as one of the eagles screeched, beat its wings and glided into the huge air space of the valley. It caught a thermal and soared up until it disappeared into the blue haze.

"Well" said Gorvy calling the meeting to order. "I'm sure that's quite enough of a story for you to take in. You must be very tired".

Nathan, as usual placed his bag under his pillow. He pulled out the priceless canvas and switched on his torch. So this was it! It was mainly dark as a picture and he felt as though he ought

136

not to be looking at it on his own. He put it back. The words of Gorvy echoed in his mind as he lay in his bed that night…. "*You are the solution to this situation….*"

Chapter Fifteen

<u>Asterix in the north</u>

<u>August 9th</u>

The early morning window showed Nathan another scene up near the Tower tree. An eagle circled high. It was a lone flier and clearly not one of the two that guarded the eyrie. It swooped down, its wings ragged, bearing the marks of previous skirmishes. Down the eagle dropped and attacked the nest. The protecting mother and father rose up to meet it resulting in a clash of talons and ripped flesh. The three eagles now regained altitude and eyed each other before attacking again. Within the eyrie, the four adolescent eagles watching this event, stretched their wings and prematurely, took their hasty maiden flights.

After breakfast in the grange barn, Jacob found another note, again lying half under the Fielding's front door. This time it was written in Peter's hand. Jacob read it out.

> *My dear Fieldings*
> *Sadly other projects have called me away; however I have*
> *made arrangements for you to engage in the next stage. Do*
> *not worry we will be with you, although you may not see us*
> *as such. The tickets are enclosed for your journey back*
> *north. It would be hugely complicated for the Panel or I to*
> *courier your temporary 'property' back to its rightful owners.*
> *To this end I have made arrangements for one of my people*
> *to meet you at the Asterix theme parc just north of Paris.*
> *There you will blend in and enjoy the facilities (no hardship*
> *here I guess) and at 2pm you must queue up for the 'Zeus'*
> *ride where you will meet Juess. He will greet you with a*
> *symbol, a code which will inform you of his authenticity. The*
> *symbol will be a ring with a fish sign upon it. Give him*
> *your special package and after the ride leave the parc and*
> *proceed quietly to le Havre where I have arranged for a*
> *private ship to take you directly to Cardiff Bay and back*
> *home............*

"The rest says about the channel instructions and how to find the ship and also a taxi to take us to Bergerac airport."

"Is today when we go to the theme park, the Aster thing?"asked Matthew. He was happy about this and after a short flight and another taxi ride the family arrived at the Asterix theme park. The buzz and excitement of the park put a spring in Matthew's step. He was hugely excited.

Time went quickly, with all the major rides bar one attempted.

"Oh Mum, it's1.30" called Matthew as he climbed off a ride.

The towering statue of Zeus soared some 30 metres into the air. His Greek styled garb and mighty axe looked impressive and set the scene for what proved to be an equally mighty ride.

"Look" said Matthew "his pants are yellow."

The six queued for a long time moving only very slowly.

"This is quite glacial "said Laura

"I wonder where I heard that before!" Jacob teased.

Eventually the half way mark in the long queue was reached.

"Oh, what's occurin' " said Jacob. Something was upsetting the other visitors behind them. "Someone's barging to the front, he's got some cheek." He paused noticing the man's large frame. The angry looks, his eyes and down turned mouth said it all. Jacob suddenly felt cold and reckoned that any challenge would be met with aggression. The queue parted reluctantly at the man's running arrival. Jacob hoped that he wasn't coming for them, but he knew he was wrong as the angry face stopped exactly by them. He looked sweaty, grim and overpoweringly strong.

"You must come with me" he said.

Nathan moved backwards instinctively, his father questioned the man,

"Who are you, you aren't Juess?". The man was annoyed that he had to prove himself so held up his hand. It was stained and on his smallest finger was the ring, inlaid with the fish sign on it. He replied,

"He couldn't make it, now come with me". Reluctantly the children's father agreed. Complaints were heard behind them as the now party of seven were holding up the queue considerably. Pressured by the crowd they all moved nearing the point where they would board the pods for the Zeus ride. Laura could see that the pods took four people each, so they split up. She made sure that the four children got into one pod, her parents and their unwelcome, suspicious guest, in the other. These were the first two of the chain of pods. As everyone clambered aboard, Laura saw quite clearly a dirty, stained, long edged knife inside the visitor's jacket as he reached out to hold onto the rails of the pod.

"Dad he's got a knife" whispered Laura, as she leant over from her pod towards her father. The impostor looked up, suspicious of the whispering. A bit of rubbish hit Mr. F on the ears and he turned around to find Laura miming a cut throat stroke.

'And we haven't started the ride yet' sighed Laura. She thought that the stains on his knife, the stains on his hand and trousers all fitted into a dreadful order. It was now clear what had happened. They were trapped in a ride, the most feared in France……… that had just started.

With a shunt, rocking and a concertina'd knocking, the train started to move. Laura looked ahead to her father, desperately silently urging him to do something and saw three levers, yellow and red and green. Inspired by the colour of Zeus's underwear, she reached out and grabbed yellow. The man immediately drew out his knife and held it to Mrs F's throat. Fortunately the yellow lever had released the pod from the main train and being the first part it accelerated like a rocket, flinging the knife into the air. The pod was now running at a huge speed. It soared up to the first peak of the track and disappeared over the top of the huge ascent. The rest of the train with the Four inside, climbed the ascent more slowly and then tipped over, freefalling down a near vertical stretch of track. Laura looked down to see her father and the thug wrestling in the first pod while it soared up to the next peak. She could see her father reaching out with one hand to pull another lever before it all disappeared out of view. Laura strained to see what was happening but could only hear the accelerating rumble of the pod rocketing down on the far side. The main section of the train rumbled slowly up to the top rise. Laura was desperate to see what had happened.

Unable to do anything, the train surged downwards. Laura gasped with the drop and at the blurred view of the first pod which had stopped at the base of this crazy drop...someone was getting out. The tracks shuddered as the remainder of the pod train with the Four on board descended at great speed towards the first pod. Being in the front, the Four screamed as they saw their parents trying to get out.

A few seconds later the train crashed into the lone pod throwing it and someone off the rails. The remainder of the train somehow hurtled on, mechanically following its preset journey back to where it had started.

Damaged and one pod less, the train drew sadly into the station to screams and mass hysteria from the waiting, queuing crowds.Laura began to shake, Jacob was shouting wildly and the other two were crying.Laura looked at the front of the pod. It had been ripped off and blood was splattered all over it. The attendants ran around in a state of panic, releasing all the safety bars. An emergency alarm rang out. Jacob was dazed and got out of his pod. An attendant came straight over and sat him and the others down on a bench offering water.

Eventually after what seemed like ages Laura spoke. "Look everyone, we don't know how mum and dad are and we've got the bag with you know what in it, and well, it might be that there are others of them around Ok?" she paused "so let's leave without anyone knowing and find mum and dad quietly."

"Are they Ok?" asked Jacob.

No one knew the answer.

"But I want them here" said Matthew

"I know" replied Laura "but if we go looking for them we might get caught by others"

"But where's mum?" Matthew was in tears

"I want dad" Nathan joined in.

Jacob desperately wanted to give in to the emotions, but he knew he needed to help the other two.

"We can't do this on our own," Nathan continued to cry and his words were barely understandable.

"I want mum" Matthew cried.

"Laura's right boys, for once!" said Jacob reluctantly.

They slipped out of the train shelter and quickly started searching.

Chapter Sixteen

<u>**Parted**</u>

"Look!" said Jacob pushing the others down under a hedge. "It's mum & dad, they've been captured." "Hide boys keep down" added Laura, but they were already hiding having seen who'd got their parents. Matt bit his lip, for a second he was happy they were alive and not crashed, but now those people were taking them away in a black car just like the one he'd seen at Christmas. He put his head down in his hands.

Laura's heart pumped hard, she knew she should take charge. "Ok well we need to get out of here quickly and not be tracked."

"What do you think is going to happen to them?" asked Nathan. Thinking it was best not to talk about it Laura replied

"I don't know Nath but we can't do anything about it"

"I want mum" Matthew was crying. Jacob put an arm around him.

"So do I Matt but they'd want us not to get caught so let's do what Laura said," thinking to himself that he couldn't believe what he heard himself saying.

"We can't go on our own" Nathan was still crying. Matthew was slumped on the floor barely consolable. For some twenty minutes the four were in a state of worry and total confusion. Matthew was crying so much that Laura had to try to silence his cries. She wanted to give up. 'I'm only twelve' she thought. She gripped herself,

"Come on, we can't let them get us." The boys agreed, or rather two of them did very reluctantly.

Skirting around the edge of the park and going through all the 'interdite' places, an exit was finally found as they slipped out of the park. The Four, worried that more of the gang would be at the main gate and avoided this by using staff entrances and other exits. Somehow they managed to leave unnoticed.

Laura knew that the next challenge was obvious, standing in the middle of a massive car park with no means of travel.

"Where's the real person" asked Nathan. "If his ring finger has been cut off, where's the rest of him, and the other finger?'

The four walked around the edge of the car park, looking for inspiration until Jacob hushed the others and stood retriever like still. They were at the closest part of the car park to the Zeus ride. A low slow groaning came from inside one of the evergreen bushes. Jacob looked into the bush to find a man collapsed, bearing one very clear identification mark. His right hand was missing a finger and dark and bloody trails were all over him.

His eyes, congealed and barely open, widened at the sight of the Four.

"Quick he's trying to say something" said Jacob who leaned closer.

"Poussez trois, deux, un" he barely whispered.

"It must be his phone." said Laura

Sure enough, reaching into his jacket, Laura retrieved a slim cell phone and pressed 3, 2, 1.The camera's inset picture showed the face of Father Jenks.

"Good afternoon, please pan the camera around Laura."

Laura was sitting down in the hedge so asked Nathan to hold the phone and carry out a full sweep around. He did this and handed it back.

"Now Laura please give me a short account of what has just happened."

Laura summed up the dramatic events on the roller coaster and now having found the real Juess, Jacob, Nathan and Matthew all chipped in with additions and corrections.

"Thank you. I will now make arrangements for Juess to be rescued; you need not do anything more for him now. I'm afraid that you must do the next bit yourselves. I understand that it must be worrying to be a way from your parents. I have sent a team to rescue them, however if we are caught with you it will be even more dangerous than you can imagine."

At this point Jacob asked angrily "Yeah like it's not been dangerous before now".

"Jacob it is vital that you now travel to Paris to the Notre Dame Cathedral. How you do it must be your own decision and a secret, so that you cannot be touched or traced. Be there tomorrow at 1pm. Goodbye."

The screen abruptly shut down and despite all attempts to switch it back on, it was of no use. Laura blurted out,

"Quick, if they are listening in to this and sending people we can't be found here. Let's go. "

Matthew hadn't quite worked things out, particularly not the urgency.

"But why Laura I….."

"No I don't understand either" she interrupted "but quick let's go over there". Laura led them to a people-carrier nearby.

"If we can find a roof box that's not locked we should be able to get out of here without being noticed."

All efforts to find a car with a big enough un-locked roof box seemed fruitless until just when tempers were becoming frayed and energies were all but gone, a car, driven hard with screeching tyres and grinding gears entered the far end of the car park. Jacob climbed desperately up another large car and opened up the roof box.

"Yes!" he shouted.

Laura grabbed Nathan, pushed him up and turned to Matthew.

"No, No" said Matthew.

"Quick we haven't got time"

"Where's mum?" he wailed.

"Matthew, we'll get caught, they'll get us."

"No I don't want to"

"Matthew please"

"No" he cried and fell to the floor "Mum".

Laura picked him up and shoved him with a huge effort up to Jacob's out-stretched hands. She climbed up the car's wing mirrors and was almost in when the screaming car shot past the parking bay. At the same time, the returning family who owned the car arrived. This family's young children were crying with tiredness. Laura froze whilst lying down in the roof box realising that this meant the possibility of pushchairs being placed in the box. The Four lay still while doors were opened up. The clattering and closing of push chairs was audible. Someone stood on the door inner sill and opened the roof box a few inches. Just then a woman said something in french, the boot opened and the roof box fell closed. Laura drew a silent sigh of relief.

Shut in the dark Nathan whispered "How do we know where they are going?"

Laura replied, "It's Ok I saw some paperwork on the dashboard which said the Ritz Paris or something, anyway hold on everyone and no more talking".

Matthew was very scared at the thought of travelling without a seat and seatbelt. The darkness was the worst and even though he couldn't stop crying, Matthew kept quiet.

After what seemed an age the car came to a stop. When the coast sounded clear Jacob tried to open the roof box.

"Come on Jacob" shouted Nathan.

"I can't, it's clicked shut"

The heat and lack of air had started to take its toll. Nathan fought off the panic of being trapped in a hot box. Jacob furiously fiddled with levers until finally a satisfying 'clunk' was heard. All arms pushed up and opened up the lid. The light and fresh air was overwhelming.

All four of them then looked around and took in the sight. Not only was the readjustment to the bright light stunning, but the whole view in front of them was amazing. Despite being in a hotel car park Jacob counted five Bentleys, six Rolls Royces, Jaguars, Mercedes, Ferraris, Limousines, BMW's just to name a few of the impressive automobiles on display. "This is a very expensive hotel."

"Yeah it looks posh" said Matthew. Glad of some relief, everyone smiled.

"Hmnn, maybe it's a good one, never heard of the Ritz Laura?" said Jacob to his embarrassed sister.

"What do we do now?" asked Matthew, who had partly cheered up. "I'm really hungry. Have you got another cunning plan?"

"Well as it happens" replied a resurgent Laura "I have. Come on boys"

And with that 'she marched confidently into the rear entrance to the world famous Paris Ritz Hotel and straight to its reception area. It was as elegant and overwhelmingly impressive a place as the boys had ever seen. They gawped and stood looking around much to Laura's embarrassment.

"Look" she said tetchily "we must not look out of place here, don't stare, and try to look cool". She strode up to the main desk where an unimpressed and sneering concierge looked down his very long and narrow nose through a gold rimmed pince-nez. In a clear voice she announced:

"We would like a room, a family room with four beds please."

The Frenchman, to whom she was talking, was incredulous. He was a very experienced member of the hotel staff and was rather taken aback by being addressed by a twelve year old girl.Accustomed as he was to looking after royalty, prime ministers, film stars and celebrities; to be asked for a room by four children was something rather beneath him.

"Er Mademoiselle, we cannot accept bookings from, er well, les enfants."

"Well" replied Laura confidently "You'll find everything is in order" she said whilst producing a credit card on the marble counter.

"Mais mademoiselle, c'est impossible".

"I think you might find the hotel embarrassed if you do not accept my request" responded Laura. The boys did not know how she had got the credit card nor knew what she was doing, since booking hotels was something not taught at school. Laura's eyes held the French receptionist who picked up the card and placed it into the machine with a disdain.The machine processed the card and the concierge had what seemed to be a 'road to Damascus' experience.

"Ah mademoiselle of course" he smiled at her and clicked his well clicked fingers. A porter arrived to show them to the room.

On the wayNathan noticed the long plush corridors and cushioned landings.

"But Laura, how have you got us in here?"Nathan asked, amazed with the gold trimmed finest antique furniture.

"Well" she replied with a smug smile, "on the Zeus ride Dad threw the wallet at me. It seems that Mr. Gorvy's credit card goes a long way."

Laura stopped and went over to hug Matthew. Mention of her father brought it back to him that they were separated from his parents. He wanted them back very much.

"Now then" resumed Laura, feeling the need to take on her mother's role. "Pile up all your clothes in this bag and I'll get them laundered as we've got no others."

The boys did as she asked and then set about having a monumental bath creating enough bubbles to fill the base of the Eiffel Tower.

"I'm starving" said Jacob, so he got the menu out.

"Let's order the expensive stuff".

When the feast arrived on two trolleys, each item covered with a huge silver dome, Matthew realised he had not got a really balanced diet, so he ordered two extra bowls of chips as well.

The three boys all piled the cushions together and made a sleeping boy's palace. Nathan took a long time to sleep. He cradled his bag under the duvet cover. During the night Matthew awoke again and went into Laura,

"I want mum" he said
"I know," said Laura, "so do I. So do I."

Chapter Seventeen

<u>Notre Dame</u>

<u>10th August</u>

*"It is not death that a man should fear, but he should fear
never beginning to live."*

A Jaguar taxi was not an uncommon sight in
central Paris. Many of its fashionable inhabitants
liked to travel in style. This one drove slowly
through the tightly packed back streets,
immediately behind the Notre Dame Cathedral
and then parked. It was quiet except for a lady clad
in a black and white fur coat being pulled by a pair
of very young but enthusiastic Dalmatian puppies.
The car's engine idled but then pulled away at
speed, in response to a cell phone call to its driver.

Jacob was woken up by what turned out to
be the highly efficient Ritz Hotel laundry service.
A little more confidence was also present in the air
as the Four enjoyed breakfast in their room.

"Let's go down" said Jacob. The furnishings still impressed Nathan on the way to the reception area. Half way down the flowing stairs Jacob stood stock still. In front of him, standing at the front desk, was the one person he did not want to see. LeClaw was handing over a wad of Euro notes to the receptionist who appeared to Jacob to be giving him a card type room key.

"Let's go back" he hissed.

Immediately, the Four ran to the room, gathered belongings but not quickly enough as the dreadful sound of those metal heeled boots was heard coming along the corridor. They pushed a sofa on to the door just in time before LeClaw unlocked it, only to find his way barred.

"And you can't come in" said Matthew. Three seconds later a crushing splintering blow came through the door panel and a metal fist stood proudly and fiercely through the wood. It quickly reached for the upper part and with amazing ease, stripped the door from inside out.

"Come on. The fire exit" shouted Jacob. "Out there Matt, to those outside stairs." Heran on to the grill likesteps and descended as fast as possible to the front of the hotel, following Laura who ran right into a waiting Jaguar taxi shouting "Vite! Notre Dame!"

Despite her panic, Laura noticed that the taxi driver did not bat an eye, which in itself was peculiar as four children commissioning a taxi from the Ritz was hardly normal. The Jaguar taxi swept off and drove swiftly through the Parisian streets until it found the cathedral's cobble stones, stopping close to its famous twin towers.

"Do you take credit cards?" Laura asked in English. The taxi driver reached down to his glove complement. "Voici" he said and pulled out a small envelope. He drove off without waiting for payment.

The boys crowded around her as Laura opened the unmarked envelope, it read;

> *'Bon jour again mes amis. On that yellow motorbike you will find directions. Ivan.'*

"Hey it's Mr. Angel the motorbike man" shouted Nathan.

All of them shared his excitement but not for long as a screeching of tyres was heard at a nearby traffic light system.

"Quick, Jacob, run to the motorbike and grab that note wedged into its saddle seat. Now come on into the cathedral," shouted Laura who thought it was almost like medieval times, seeking sanctuary from a pursuing enemy. By the light of a bright group of candles and accompanied by a choir far off in an echoing end of the cathedral, Jacob read the note;

"Climb the bell-tower, basically" he said. Avoiding buying tickets, the Four ran up the steps and arrived in the great bell chamber. This time, instead of a hunchback, the first rescuer Ivan Furle stood waiting. They were overjoyed to meet him but he had no smile.

"Well done mes amis but we must make progress. You have been followed and even now LeClaw's men are in the cathedral." said the serious Ivan. "I had hoped to escort you to a safe rendezvous to hand over the picture."

"What happened to Father Jenks?" said Laura "He's supposed to meet us."

"Ah well, he is preaching even as we speak in the cathedral below, so he called me in".

"But why can't you take it now?" cried Nathan who began to fill up, over come with the mental burden of the contents of his rucksack.

"No" Ivan was adamant, "I am sorry it's just...it's just that..." Ivan hesitated. Laura could see in his face the enormity of the temptation for him. It passed by and he looked resolute again. "I must not touch it.It is absolutely imperative mes amis".

"The Panel do much great work but can't be seen to be involved in this matter; to be seen to be part of it will undermine the heroic deeds being done elsewhere where other evil people are being dealt with. The picture must be returned by you. Now I have arranged a taxi to take you to the

Eiffel Tower, I cannot tell you what will happen there, but you must go to the top section, level three and wait for someone you know in the café."

"But if LeClaw's people are here" asked Nathan "how can we get out?"

"Do not worry" said Ivan "come with me."

The Four climbed more old stairs and went through doors and wooden galleries that were clearly not open to the public. Nathan was overwhelmed by the deep, dusty darkness that surrounded him. Years of history could be tasted in his throat. After what seemed an age, he looked out to the open air and the roof that spanned the length of the Cathedral and at a point which dipped like a 'V'

"Quick" urged Ivan, "go now to the end. Follow the groove then first right, then first left until you come to a wooden door at the far end. Open it, descend and then take the right hand door at the base which will open to the outside. The same taxi that brought you will be waiting. Go now!"

And with that Ivan showed them all out and shut the door behind them.

"Quick Matt, don't wait" said Jacob.

The Four clambered on until they reached the end of the first section where they turned right, continued for ten metres and then paused. The roof shape had now changed from an inverse shape to a conventional shape and the only way to the wooden door that Ivan had mentioned, was along the ridge. Matthew started to scrunch his eyes up; no tears but just fright.

"It's Ok" said Laura. "Matt you've done worse than this, remember when dad took us to the Lake District and we did that nightmare ridge called Striding Edge on Hellvellyn. You did that OK didn't you?"

"But dad held my hand all the way and he's not here now" replied Matthew. Laura realised that this was a good argument, but she battled on.

"Ok Matt but you're bigger and stronger now, hold my hand."

Matthew opened his eyes, pursed his lips and crawled on, desperately gripping roof tiles with his whole body. Carefully he picked his way along the ancient ridge with the twin towers now behind. Reaching out he dislodged a tile; it slid scuttling down to the left.

"Quick get down" said Laura. They all lay out like crabs on the ridge and waited a good two minutes. Nothing had happened so the journey continued even more carefully. Eventually the wooden door was reached but before entering, Matthew looked over the parapet.

"Matt, don't do that someone might see you" nagged Laura whispering.

"Ok" he replied, realizing he was wrong but not wanting to admit it. "There's no car down there".

Nathan tapped him on the shoulder,

"Listen" he said "there's no option."

In the distance, they could hear the sound of roof slates being dislodged without care. The cluttering sounds came from the now far off roof section of the cathedral that they had just scaled. The tiles were coming off in great numbers which meant only one thing. The Four bolted through the door and down the stairs to the base.Nathan opened the wrong door to see one of LeClaw's people who looked up. The man instantly broke into a run and grabbed his cell phone.

"Nathan!" shouted Jacob "Shut it". He did so, followed the others out of the correct exit and ran to the waiting taxi, with doors strangely and fortuitously open. The Four piled in and without conversation the driver accelerated away at pace. Being no other exit than the one at the front of the cathedral, the Jaguar slammed through bollards and cones and screeched onto the main road causing chaos, consternation and an orchestra of irate French car horns.

"Belts on" said Laura who had been thrown into the foot well. The car swerved and skidded. Three black Mercedes caught up with them, as well as several chasing police cars.

The Jaguar followed the banks of the river Seine trying to escape its hunters until it reached the traffic lights which stood beneath the huge Eiffel Tower. The driver screeched across red traffic lights and more barriers. The engine screamed out as they accelerated right underneath the Eiffel Tower's huge base that was swarming with tourists around each huge leg. The Jaguar slammed on its brakes at a far corner and blocked an entrance to the pedestrian 'walk up only' stanchion of the world famous tower.

"Follow me," the driver shouted in a very clipped English accent, one they knew but couldn't place. He got them to the ticket gate throwing each one over then disappeared. "Get to the top" were the last words they heard from him.

"That was Dan" shouted Matthew who was madly scampering up the steps and counting each one as he went.

"What the man in Mr. Gorvy's tower?" said a breathless Nathan.

"Just run you two!" shouted Laura who had realized that her pursuers had now also started the climb both by the stairs and by lift.

"We're trapped" said Jacob.

Laura kept running but only because she had no other plan. Above or below, either way they were in peril. 'If someone who hadn't even got the Mona Lisa had a finger chopped off, what would the Movement do to four children who had possession of it?' she worried.

Deafening alarm bells began to ring. The crowds on the tower instantly began running down its four legs. Laura could feel herself panicking, her heart pumping. She noticed that some heavily booted men were now ascending the metal grilled stairway from below. Above her, the surging wave of people coming down was an impossible wave to break through. Laura stood still. She saw an electric power unit with a door going into it and tried the handle but it was locked solidly. This was it. It was all over. Holding back the tears, holding the boys to her sides, they gripped each other waiting for the inevitable double tide to wash over them. The wait was too much.

'Finish us now' thought Laura.

Matthew broke free of Laura's hand and squeezed through a low gap in one corner of the stair well. The upper part of the grilled metal mesh moved upwards to allow him in and he called out to the others. Despite not knowing where it went Laura considered it heaven compared to the alternative. The Four all squeezed through and just in time, for the descending crowds and LeClaw's men stumped past just seconds later, the men shouting and breathing foul French language. The Four desperately clambered down along a narrow meshed walkway which opened up at the corner of the massive high tower of metal and bolts. Here there were no friendly safety rules. A mere sign separated them from the plunge and free-fall that was next to them. Nathan made the mistake of looking down and went through the mental imagination of falling forever.

A buzzing noise burst into earshot. Laura looked across to the other side of the tower and then looked up. The descending crowds had nearly cleared. She could hear the men shouting angrily, they seemed to be at the place on the stairway where they had crawled out. Matthew gripped the stanchion hard until it hurt in an attempt to cope with the tension of being hunted. Nathan was undisturbed and peered into the darkness, while Jacob pulled his head down and grimaced at Nathan. Laura just lay on the cold metal grills. She breathed heavily, her heart thumping and like Matthew tightly gripped a 'v' shaped rail.

She could hear much shouting and the men appeared to be splitting up, 'probably hunting in pairs' she thought. A torch beam probed very close by. Matthew grabbed hold of Laura and buried his head into her. The torch beam wandered around the corner, feeling its way along empty walkways, looking, searching like an angry snake, robbed of its 'kill'. Nathan's head popped up again and caught the beam full in his face. The men shouted out to the others but were drowned out by the buzzing noise which had now become deafening. Laura looked up. 'A helicopter, was it Dan?' The Paris light was fading. Someone waved from the cockpit in front of her. The Four waved and the pilot acknowledged but did not stop, accelerating up to the top of the tower.

"Why doesn't he help us?" asked Matthew. Laura looked up and could tell that the helicopter had attracted the attention of the gang. The helicopter buzzed around the top of the tower for some time. She craned her neck upwards trying to work out what it was doing, but could only see the beamed light pointing upon one part of the upper section. It then moved sharply downwards down, down towards her. A huge roar deafened her ears and a blinding beam hit her suddenly as a powerful second helicopter rushed upwards across her view. This second helicopter looked menacing and its twin torch beams were not so much finding them but hunting them down. Despite the dazzling power of the lights, Jacob shouted out

"Look ropes are being dropped and men sliding down from the other helicopter." Once at the end of the ropes and then working up a pendulum like swing, the new invaders were inching closer towards the stanchion, to get near to them. Jacob could tell that the safe gap that the helicopter had left from the tower meant that several swings were required to get close. As the

Four cowered down, Jacob panicked, he was trapped 'like a prisoner waiting to be shot 'he thought.

Laura shrieked as one 'rope man' made contact but his hands slipped and fell away. Another man grabbed a part of the metal stanchion right by her feet which triggered off an effective stamp from Jacob sending the second rope man cursing in mid air. He felt better, glad he was still able to do something.

"There's Dan's helicopter" shouted Nathan. He looked at the two machines, just like two angry mechanical wasps hovering and then to his great fright, shooting at each other. Gunfire from the helicopters spat at each other, bullets ricocheted off the ironwork around them.

Meanwhile, Laura had put her hands over her eyes, she knew this was it. She could crack under the terror of being a helpless target from random bullets or she could keep the boys going. She clung close to the latter only by a slim wisp of will power left.The gun fire was unbearably loud and frightened her beyond anything she'd ever experienced. The battle noise grew massively. It was a nightmare hung in midair until….. BANG, a huge fireball came from the second helicopter. The noise of its rotors now whirred with a lower, sickeningly lurching sound. It dropped 50 yards beneath them and slid on to a stanchion. The rotors severed off in a shower of sparks and became engulfed in flames, whilst its tail wedged in between a forked section of the tower's ironwork. She looked down at the now clipped rotor spine and thought it looked like a vast spider, de-legged and stuttering for life. The remains of the helicopter slid further down the side of the tower in lurches, held on by broken pieces of twisted metal. She could just make out its pilot scrambling out of the smashed screen, one hand gripping the tower's leg.

Dan lowered his helicopter and spoke to them via its PA system.

"Run quickly to the lift and up to the top balcony!"

Laura sensed the need to acknowledge this and gave thumbs up. She urged the boys to turn and crawl back to the stairs, desperately hoping the men had gone from the main stairway. Her worries were groundless. The gang appeared to have either been slaughtered or vanished in the helicopter battle. The Four ran to the top of level one, crossed and slipped into the lift which was now empty. Laura pressed the third level button. Quickly the doors shut and it zoomed swiftly up, up, up by-passing level two, and up and up as if it now were ascending a mere bean pole, high up above the Paris night air. Higher and higher the lift travelled giddyingly up as the neck of the tower became almost the width of the lift.

Laura felt giddy and held onto Matt. Nathan pressed himself against the compartment and gripped his bag.

Finally the lift stopped and let them out onto a deserted tourist viewing gallery. Here they ran, finding Dan hovering in his helicopter on the other side.

"Take the rope" the amplified voice sounded.A rope swung wildly in the wind several times before Jacob grabbed it after three tries, but then dropped it. He'd been jolted by the screeching, sliding, scraping shuddering of the tower.

Nathan looked over the edge and grabbed at the iron work desperately as his legs collapsed. Far below, the damaged helicopter had broken free from its wedged hold and was plummeting down metal on metal, down to the ground. It exploded at the foot of the corner nearest the river Seine and sent up a huge ball of fire, which even though some distance from him, singed his eyebrows, blinding him for a few moments. The massive deep groaning and grinding that followed, were as though some monster mother had begun the labour pains of childbirth. Then, below and around them, the gnashing and snapping of wires, rivets and stanchions all joined in, as section by section of the tower became unstable. Laura shook with this gruesome symphony, as jolts and vibrations rattled through the soles of her feet. This woeful music continued quickly and grew into the shuddering of an earthquake. The Four were high, high up, perched in the sky on top of the enormous and now leaning Eiffel Tower. The very foundations of the Parisian monument were rocking, struggling, shaking.

The noise became louder and louder. Laura shouted but no one could hear her through the destruction and smashing all around. All four suddenly fell and grabbed the moving floor as a massive jolt rocked the platform. They grasped at anything to steady them. Laura was standing on a woken volcano, ready to erupt, metal work vibrating like a demented engine. The floor was now at a steep angle. She fell. The huge splitting sounds of screaming metalwork twisting and bending were unbearable. The platform slowly subsided, leaning to the left. The world famous Tour D 'Eiffel was slowly collapsing beneath them. Another huge jolt sent them sliding as the platform tilted again, lurching further.

Laura looked up at the helicopter hovering almost above them such was the angle of tilt. A cable with attachments swung from the helicopter and into her reach.

"Quick" shouted Laura desperately "all hold on to the handles."

And this they did, interlocking arms together like a nest of fledglings wrapped together in a huddle. The platform fell away and all eight hands and arms took their full weight. The helicopter's winch turned slowly. Laura's hands held on like claws and she looked down. The tower now slipped away, and then, it went. Falling as a huge statue of twisted metal and snapping framework dying all at the same time into the river below.

The night air seemed to disappear as the four arrived at the end of the winch and were bundled quickly to safety whilst the hatch closed. Collapsed, they lay on the side of the helicopter, half watching the massive crash as the proud sunflower of France exploded into the mighty river Seine, now its watery grave.

Chapter Eighteen

<u>Grunters</u>

<u>11th August</u>

"And here we have this truly shocking and amazing scene…Incredibly only ten people died……..A mystery helicopter battle…And now back to the CNN studio……"
"From the BBC we bring you the latest……"

A large TV……breakfast news, speaking….in English….The news… when dad watches at breakfast… Laura's mind flowed in and out of consciousness. Her head lay deep in a soft silken pillow and her legs stretched out in a massive bed. In and out of a nightmare she drifted. Huge explosions, thundering helicopters…..hanging on, bullets….falling, falling…..the boys, the boys where are they? She drifted…..
Laura sat upright and couldn't believe her eyes. A very large, elegantly decorated and

furnished bedroom was before her. An expansive bay window looked out onto sweeping, manicured lawns, which were vivid green and immaculate. At the far end of the lawn was a lake, edged on one side with ancient oaks.Laura found a dressing gown and wrapped it around her. The images of last night were beginning to make sense. She opened the door, found a long landing and heard familiar voices. The boys!

The boys were talking and laughing. When Laura walked in she ran and, quite uncharacteristically, hugged them, remembering how they had all survived a horrifying ordeal. For a while all they could talk about was the wall to wall coverage of the crashed Eiffel Tower.

A butler appeared at the door.

"Ahem" he announced, "breakfast is served lady and gentlemen."

Confused but smiling, they followed the butler, who walked smoothly down an extravagant staircase and into the breakfast room.

"You beauty" said Jacob. He was starving. Rashers of bacon, sausage, toast, marmalade, cereals, hash browns, fried eggs, tomatoes and juice all made up the feast.

After breakfast the butler reappeared.

"His lordship will see you now".

They walked into a library with books on shelves that went right up to the ceiling in all directions. Nathan carried his backpack with him, it rarely left his side. A log fire was burning and leather sofas were on three sides. A piano finished playing in a nearby room. A familiar voice boomed out:

"Ah Mozart's Sonata in D, my favourite piece". Lord Gruntfuttock strolled in; 'the very personification of cheeriness' thought Jacob.

"Aha how splendid, how absolutely marvellous to see you four again. My! What a rip roaring adventure you've had." Jacob was amazed by the enthusiasm and happiness of the man which was enormous. Not to mention his waistline. He shook each one of the children by the hand and then took up what was obviously a familiar position by the mantelpiece.

"Ah that's better" he sat on his armchair next to them. "Very well done indeed, yes it's reminded me of back in '85 when I was in India" he chortled and looked out longingly through the windows. "Anyway how about you four, have you recovered from last night?"

Jacob considered this for a while and said,

"We've been on the run for the best part of a week, been separated from our parents, been shot at in a mid air battle, escaped from the collapsing Eiffel Tower and now wake up to a massively cheery ('and fat' he thought) English Lord, who by settling down to a good pipe by the fire, thinks a good night's sleep hasmeant that we are all recovered...".

"Of course you're not," continued Lord Gruntfuttock "don't worry I'm not completely bonkers you know. Now then don't worry about mum and dad, I've got Dan and Kim on the case and they are making progress. Very good man Dan you know, good cricketer he was, don't know Kim so well, not sure if she ever played cricket ..." Grunters stopped,

"....oh, well, anyway where was I eh? I guess you could all do with a good rest yes? Good, well my butler Fewings will sort you out".

Grunters stood up, wished them well and said that he'd see them later at lunch.

Over lunch, all four of the children grilled Fewings about his background, which broke down his serious appearance. Fewings had seemed a bit stand-offish to Jacob, but now that they had shown an interest in him, the Butler warmed to their enthusiasm. He regaled them with stories of his army days, how he had carried out some very important and secret work in Ireland, Thailand, Afghanistan and other places he "couldn't possibly mention" (but did). It was at this point that he became somewhat misty eyed and stopped somewhat abruptly.

"What is it Fewings?" asked Laura intuitively.

"Well my wife, she, she was taken, kidnapped, never seen again, I don't know if she is alive or………"

His words faltered, Laura went up to him placing a hand on his shoulder.

"How long ago?" she asked.

"Oh a long time now, er nearly forty years ago in London on our way to our honeymoon. Anyway let's put on wellies and waxed jackets and go for a ride in the Landrover over the highlands".

Seven chimes of the grandfather clock preceded the sound of a large gong booming out in the main oak panelled hallway. Nathan put his backpack under his pillow again. The boys ran out of their bedroom and slid down the stairs in a heap, using the wide banister as a slide. Laura looked on with some disdain, but greeted Fewings warmly. Lord Gruntfuttock was standing by the fire warming a rather special claret in his crystal wineglass.

"Ah good evening" he announced in his booming voice. "I hear you had a jolly good day what?"

"Nathan, let's get stuck into some pheasant we caught on the estate yesterday, you'll enjoy it with a rather vintage blackcurrant juice I've been saving."

The boys liked his blackcurrant joke and joined in the fun.

"Ah yes Grunters" replied Jacob sniffing his cut glass crystal tumbler.

"A rather nice nose and undertones of woodiness I think."

Nathan didn't want to miss out.

"I would agree dear brother, a rather fruity number."

Grunters enjoyed the banter "…you don't say, that's splendid quite splendid." They all laughed and even six year-old Matthew chipped in;

"A nice red colour on it" as he lifted his glass to the red firelight.

"Well, now let's eat" concluded Grunters as Fewings began to carve and serve. "Who's to say Grace?" he asked and, quick as a flash, Nathan offered.

"Now I wanted to talk to you about how we are to conclude your little adventure," said his Lordship.

"If this is little, I'd like to see a big one" quipped Jacob.

"So" retorted Grunters "now then, last night you will recall Dan had to go to the top of the tower first before he rescued you in the helicopter." This was a point Laura had kept in her mind. "Well the whole idea of meeting at the top of that place was to rendezvous with a very senior French government official. This gentleman was to be the person who would not blow our cover, nor prosecute."

"Prosecute?" asked Laura frustratedly "Prosecute! After all we've done?"

Matthew asked Jacob what the word 'prosecute' meant and he told him.

"Good question my dear," replied Lord Gruntfuttock "as you can imagine, all of France is pretty outraged. Its most famous work of art stolen from underneath the President's nose and the fact that a group of children had just returned it having been separated from their parents and avoiding a gang of crooks seemed, well, fairly unlikely."

"Yeah, but why can't you, the Panel, give yourselves away?" asked Jacob who couldn't understand why they still had to get the picture back.

"The Panel, as you'll recall from when we first met in the tree house in the Dordogne, is absolutely certain that it must not be compromised in its name or its whereabouts so it can continue to do good works and correct evil people."

"How do you mean compromise?" asked Nathan.

"Well it means that if people or governments know who we are and where we are, we would be pressurised to do things we might not be happy with and more importantly, other future criminals might see us as a threat and try to get rid of us. We in the Panel are quite simply invisible. Various governments and intelligence agencies…….."

Jacob leaned over to Matthew and whispered, "He means spies."

"…..know of us, but not who we are, or where we are. They tend to communicate via newspaper advertisements. We respond if we think it's reasonable and possible. Those of us who are in the Panel have a reason to be so. Some past sadness which has motivated us perhaps or….." Lord Gruntfuttock hesitated briefly and then continued,

".. of course we are richly blessed in material wealth which is how we sustain what we do. Anyway…"

Grunters paused again to enjoy another large gulp of his claret.

"…we are working on another contact. This time it is someone who has excellent links into the French arts world, someone who will be able to complete the task at hand. The only issue is how we get you, the picture and this gentleman together."

"Who is he?" asked Laura.

"He's part French and part British and is called Hal Fox. He is…"

"The renowned actor who has appeared on the West End as well as several Hollywood films?" suggested Laura.

"I see you have heard of him then!" continued Gruntfuttock. The boys look at each other in complete ignorance whilst Laura, impatient to find out more, carried on with Lord Gruntfuttock.

"He is currently appearing in Les Misérables at the Queen's Theatre in London's West End"

"Yes as Javert the….." Grunters tried to continue but Laura carried on…

"…hated police officer," continued Laura who noticed that Matthew was becoming grumpy and not understanding anything.

"Who's that and how do you know?" he asked.

"Oh well, we went to see it on a school trip last year, anyway he's a bad guy in a musical onstage in London".

"You are well informed I must say" said Lord Gruntfuttock taking another gulp. "Well I've made arrangements; tomorrow Fewings will put you on the London sleeper train, just after tea time. You will arrive in London in the morning and then check in to the Dorchester Hotel. Fewings will be with you at all times until later that day when you go into the Queen's Theatre, to link up with Mr. Fox. I should urge you to take care, particularly if you are suspicious of anything about the mission. I know you are desperately keen to be relieved of your heavy burden Nathan; however we are not fully confident about this chap. He's not had a complete background check and there are some parts of his history we are not yet aware of."

"How shall we meet him?" asked Jacob. Gruntfuttock continued,

"Good question," he hesitated again "you will have four tickets booked in a box; it's next to the Royal Box. Ten minutes before the end you will need to access Fox's dressing room. Fox and other celebrities have been invited to Buckingham Palace later that night after the performance, to meet, er lots of very important people. I should add that the French President is also in residence that evening at Buckingham Palace. As a consequence of this he will have very little time. He has been briefed that he will be given a package of special significance for the French people. It's not difficult to guess I suppose what it might be, however he will not be expecting four children."

Jacob was confused. "Ok, so how do we get to the dressing room without anyone stopping us?"

"Er, what's your acting like?" quizzed the now playful Grunters.

The Four looked at each other. Laura was relieved that it was not an Eiffel Tower sort of mission, but nervous of what was unveiling.

"Ok Grunters, let's have it then, I can see that mischievous look on your face" demanded Jacob.

"You see the thing is, the only way of accessing his dressing room is via the stage, you'll never get through backstage". Grunters hesitated knowing that the next bit would be a difficult sell. "Well" he continued "Fewings will prepare you for this. After the interval you will need to be dressed up and have applied makeup."

"Oh no boys" said Laura "we going on the stage."

"What?!" said all the boys in amazement.

"Will there be many in the crowd?" asked Nathan.

"Oh yes" replied Gruntfuttock "a full house, about 1,000 people."

The Lord looked at the four shocked, nervous and incredulous young people. "Yes a full house! You will enter the 'cast only' door at the foot of the stairwell beside your box, taking care not to let anyone see you. You'll then open the door and run into the general cast dressing room, where the other children will be ready for the barricades scene. You will need to spread out so as not to be noticed as an odd group. Mix in and then when the stage manager gives the childrenthe cue, you will need to join in and pass the barricades onto the other side of the stage."

As Grunters was describing the plan. He could see four mouths opening slightly wider. "Take care as the barricades move on a motorized base. You must get to the other side. From there the stars' dressing rooms are in front of you. Go into Fox's room and hide, awaiting his return."

It was quiet for thirty seconds. Eventually Laura concluded,

"Not much then!"

"Ha, ha my dear not much!" exclaimed the jovial lord. "Now then top up your tumblers with the vintage stuff and let's go in to the drawing room."

Laura collapsed after a very satisfying meal onto a luxurious leather sofa in front of a roaring fire, gazing deeply into the orange and red glow as the logs occasionally fell and shifted with a spark or two running up the wide chimney. The lord placed himself in between the Four and the fire and settled into his armchair with some old stories.

"Now then where was I in that story? Oh yes, India, in '85, it was very hot out there. Those dragonflies were enormous and we played to a huge crowd in Madras or what they call it now, oh yes Chennai. Letting off firecrackers all the time, quite an experience for young man I can tell you." He paused to look up.

All four were fast asleep

"Fewings" he shouted.

12th August

The following day was spent in the big house exploring its rooms and grounds until Fewings asked them all to pack. The Silver Shadow Rolls Royce swept away as Nathan looked out of its side windows and watched the Lord waving wildly.

"I've always wanted to go on a sleeper train," announced Laura.

"Trains don't sleep" stated Matthew and they all fell about laughing. The first class section had been laid out for dinner as they climbed on board.

"Woah" said Jacob "I like the look of this".

Dinner was full of laughter as the train rocketed along in excess of 100 miles an hour. Mountains and waterfalls, sheep and dry stonewalls, lakes and villages, motorways and canals, fields and fields, with the occasional shudder as another express came thudding past in the opposite direction; all sped past Nathan's eyes until the darkness came and tiredness overcame him. Finding the sleeping quarters, the Four talked long into the night. Nathan placed his backpack under his pillow. The bag had become a burden, but he did not want to give it up.

<u>13th August</u>

Fewings woke the Four. Sizzling bacon, the River Thames, boats, houses, lawns drinking from the flowing waterside and then the intercom told them that they were fifteen minutes from London.

The automatic door opened to reveal the large expanse of London's Euston station. Laura immediately froze. A wave of cold surged over her, hair on end and a feeling of deep worry woke in the pit of her stomach. Her mouth dried up so much that it was almost impossible to speak the words…

"Oh no" she cried "it's him"

"Quick" said Fewings "to the front." Fewings knew that one of the advantages of travelling first class is that one has the shortest walk to get to the ticket gate. Scuttling to the end of the first carriage, Nathan wondered how they were to get out of this. It was then that he was met by a large pack of hugely muscled and very smartly attired men.

"It's the Welsh rugby team" announced Jacob, "look that's Garin Davies the Welsh captain."

"And that's Chris Jones," added Fewings "the hardest man alive."

"How do you........." Stuttered Jacob as the Butler shouted out.

"Hey Jonesy, remember when we pushed you over at Twickenham?"

The carriage went silent. Despite it being 30 years ago, the Welsh nursed old wounds deeply, especially a 63 - nil thrashing by England.

"Now, look you Grandad" said one of the front row players whose strength and looks were rather like an ugly troll. Fewings was hoisted up by his lapels against the side of the carriage, pressed in by some very large units in jackets. The Four stood stock still.Not only was there a great danger outside, Fewings had offended an entire international rugbyteam. Then in a broad Rhondda accent, a voice came from the rear of the now brooding scrum of players surrounding Fewings,

"Well now man, if it's not old Fewings! Drop him boys. This one, was not only there, he scored three tries and pushed us over our line in the scrum as he says. He was class he was."

"You played rugby for England?" asked the amazed Jacob.

"Good to see you, you misery!" continued Jones "Well, well I remember that day well and the night after man.Anyway what are you doing coming in here? It's the end of the line?"

"Ah yes" agreed Fewings "we are in a bit of a pickle. A word please?"

The two spoke in whispers with furtive looks outside the windows.

"No problem at all, now then…………." announced the welsh man whose physical properties Jacob thought resembled that of a large fridge. Laura was very nervous, even with the private army they had fortuitously come across.

"Right" announced Fewings "be brave and follow the team who will give you protection". The squad and its new recruits disembarked from the train, being the last to leave as a consequence of the reunion. The darkly clad and pale faced LeClaw stood silently. The squad had been well drilled forming a phalanx around the Four. Fewings had disassociated himself by leaving the train amongst the last few stragglers and busied himself with a copy of the Telegraph newspaper. He knew his old friend, who had he hadn't seen in 30 years, now carried responsibility for the protection of the Four. Fewings cleared the ticket counter and did not give in to the temptation of a betraying backward look. His personal fear was palpable. Sweat dripped from his neck and forehead. He had exposed the Four to their great enemy, even to the extent of being within a few feet of him. He now trusted the might of the Welsh rugby pack and disappeared around the corner of the station, hailing a taxi. Fewings slumped into the car and it sped off. Hewas distraught that he had abandoned his precious cargo.

Chapter Nineteen.

London.

"If you are distressed by anything external, the pain is not due to the thing itself, but to your own estimates of it, and this you have the power to revoke at any moment."

Deep in London's West End, a cab pulled into Shaftsbury Avenue, the fare got out, paid the driver and, before entering one of the many theatres, took a call on his cell phone.

"Yes I have been contacted…..No that's fine I will do that……Yes no- one knows…No, it will be very late;….. I will……. we have another performance later……………..I will do".

At Euston, the children stepped off the train. This was Laura's worst nightmare. LeClaw spotted them instantly and marched angrily towards them. The closest Welsh rugby player went to stop him; however LeClaw beat him off easily with his metal hand. This surprised the next two who shouted.

"Quick boys!"

LeClaw easily disposed of these two, even though each weighed eighteen stone of muscle. His speed of hand and its weapon like quality cut them down in a heap. Laura's stomach plunged. No Fewings. This was it. She smelt LeClaw's foul breath as he lifted his metal fist...

A celtic cry was heard from the rear, followed by a roar of men who crashed into a pack like scrum. The roar, gaining volume, had distracted the raised claw. The moment of hesitation was enough for the mighty charging wave of welsh giants who slammed him into the ground. The children stood still, shocked. Nathan clung on tightly to his bag.

In the ensuing fracas, Jones, who had hailed the 'Hywl' call to arms, swiftly escorted the Four past the barrier and out of the station, onto the main road and down the side street where the taxi and heavily sweating Fewings were waiting.

"We're staying at the Regal Hotel" shouted Jones as the taxicab gathered speed leaving him wondering if he would see his old friend again. A thumb popped out the window as the cab screeched around the next corner, merging into the dense London traffic. Jones, on re-entering the station, had to disappear swiftly into a photo booth as he saw the enraged LeClaw running at full tilt, blood on his head and hands. He looked ahead to the platform and when the coast was clear joined his squad.

"What a marvellous occasion!" he announced..He knew Fewings had been unable to say why he'd mysteriously dropped out of top-line rugby, but knew there had to a good reason. He was pleased to have helped his old friend.

The Dorchester Hotel just off Regents Park, is deep in the centre ofLondon's Mayfair, where major hotels bristle with prestige and, as Nathan observed, were the most expensive streets in the game of Monopoly. He looked across the soft green sweeps of Hyde Park and remembered how his father had told him that the Dorchester was 'one of the best in the world for magnificent dining and luxury', but all he wanted to do was to hide in the bedroom after another desperate experience.

A London church bell rang out four o'clock bringing the children out of their dreams and all back to reality.

"Are you going to ask him?" Jacob asked Laura.

Laura nodded. His lordship's butler sensed that this was important and stopped what he was doing...

"Er, well, the thing is, we are grateful for what the Panel is doing for us, but well, our mum and dad, we want to see them again, so while we aren't going on strike, as such, well Matthew, well er, we really need to know something…." she faltered.

"I'm awfully sorry," responded Fewings after some time. "It's my fault I should have told you. Dan has been on the case, so to speak, and whilst we have not yet retrieved your parents, we know they are alive. They are under surveillance and our colleagues will be determining when the time is right to rescue them. Don't worry," he continued "they are in good hands."

And with that he left abruptly, perhaps so they could not question him.

Five minutes later he returned with a look in his eye, one which they had not seen before. He had gone into army mode, as Jacob was later to point out.

"Right let's get prepared," he announced and asked them all to sit around the lounge area of the suite. He continued, "We will shortly take a taxi to the Queen's Theatre. Upon arrival, proceed quickly and as unobtrusively as possible to your box using these tickets."

Fewings distributed the tickets.

"I'll have them" said Laura who took the boys' tickets off them and safely placed them in her personal bag. Fewings continued,

"At the interval you do not leave your box, in fact do not leave it for any reason until the allotted time. Use the interval to change into these costumes."

"What are they?" asked Matthew. Nathan rummaged around and answered,

"They are beggars' outfits".

"Quite so," continued Fewings, "you must remain unobserved. Halfway through the second half you'll hear a rousing chorus, just before the barricades are brought on. Put your mobile phone onto mute. You must check it visually during the second half. At the agreed moment, move from your box to the doorway marked 'staff only'. Through it you will find a stairway. Take the stairway down and turn left along the corridor. You'll find a door marked 'Stage right'. Open it slowly and judge the opportune time to enter first the corridor and then the stage."

"Stage?" exclaimed Nathan "are we going on the stage?"

"Oh Nathan, don't you listen to anything?" sighed Laura.

"And you judge when to enter the stage by merging with the other child beggars. You must climb over the main barricade taking care as it will rotate. Having scaled it and descended down the other side, you'll need to run across the stage trying to fit in."

"How do we fit in?" asked Jacob.

Good question," replied Fewings, "you'll have to try and copy others and be a bit dramatic, or join in with the singing. Anyway once you have got to the other side, go through the left wing and look for a series of silver doors where the stars of the show have their dressing rooms. Fox's name will be on one of them. Hide in his room and wait for his return. When he is alone in his room you must reveal yourselves and ask the code question."

"What's that?" asked Matthew.

"Have you seen Mr. Figsy Foghorn tonight?" replied the butler, a little embarrassed by such a strange question. And he must respond with; "Yes and I'd love to eat a jar of pickled onions."

Initially there was a rather embarrassed silence, followed by giggling and then laughing. The release of tension was very welcome. Fewings continued.

"If this has been completed satisfactorily you should hand over the bag and its precious contents."

"What's he going to do with it?" asked Jacob.

"Well" responded the aging butler "and this is absolutely top secret, hush, hush, mum's the word."

"Is mummy going to be there?" chirped Matthew.

"Ah well not as such; anyway, as you know, Fox is going to Buckingham Palace after the show. His mission is to place the picture in safe hands."

"Whose would they be?" asked Laura.

The butler hesitated, looking uncomfortable with the next part.

"Come on Fewings you are asking a lot of us, making us do all the stuff that's happened so far and tonight's show is hardly normal, we're only six, eight, ten and twelve you know?!"

Laura knew she had him and so did he. The old butler looked conspiratorially, bent his head in his direction and whispered "the safest."

"Has someone got big hands?" asked Matthew. The others ignored him but were stunned and just beginning to realize what he was saying.

"Well, are you saying what I'm thinking you are?"Laura asked

"Ah yes, I guess that what I said made you think something and I think that you are thinking of the actual person that I am thinking of!"

The butler was clearly desperate not to name names. Laura added,

"We'll take that as a yes then."

Matthew was now desperate to enter the secret.

"Who is he talking about Laura?"

Laura turned and cupped a hand to his ear and whispered. Matthew's face changed like an exaggerated cartoon. His eyes bulged and his mouth was agape.

"The Q…" Fewings quickly silenced the young boy. It was at this point that Nathan also realized as to who it was and gasped.

"I will then arrange for a car to collect you from backstage."

The Butler stood up tall and braced his shoulders with a distant look in his eye.

"Your duty will be done."Then, with almost a hint of a marching drill about-turn, he went about his other business and left the children.

Jacob bit his lip, wondering what madness was to come.

Chapter Twenty

<u>**Enter stage right.**</u>

The light had all but gone as a heavy sky with leaden grey cumulonimbus clouds had slipped over central London during the afternoon. With the change in air pressure, there was the heightened feeling of expectancy in the Capital. In a small booth by a heavily protected main gate, two policemen were talking.

"Looks like rain I bet," said a junior policeman checking his guest list.

"Forecasters say it's coming sometime." replied his boss. "Now have you looked at that list yet? Who are we expecting tonight?"

"Yes Guv, some actors or something, anyway we'll have to check 'em all just as normal I guess, that'll take some time….."

In the hotel, Laura looked out of the window. The oncoming storm, the oncoming show, both seemed to herald of heavy happenings... She pulled out the leather booklet she had picked up at Christmas and her eyes caught a poem entitled 'Autumn':

Winds tug hedge fringes, bending in the blow,
Stubbled fields lay empty now the party's gone,
Catching golden leaves in-razored rows.
Is now the time to turn over a new one?
Maybe but each day draws on quickly
Hedges heave heavily in berry bright fruit
But not for long the wild man of the night
Will shake and rattle, have his fill.
So too, frightened birds nervously pecking, always checking.
A football match finishes lost seven nil.
Not all hedges are a plenty,
Even nettles lose their summer sting.
A two furrowed pool-fested, drenched mud lane leads to,
A tired and stiff-rustling corn field
Hemmed in by hawthorns, bending buddleia and squabbling starlings.
So, capture each moment, seize the day,
And gather ye blackberries whilst ye may!

"Right" announced the butler, cutting the heaviness and collective drifting of minds with his brisk vigour. "Let's do it."

The TV went off. Fewings gathered their equipment, Nathan put his bag on his back, Laura checked her bag for the tickets.

"Ok, you may need these" said the butler as he handed out four small envelopes which contained something rectangular and flat.

"Is it a special piece of electronic equipment to help us if we have a problem?" asked Jacob. Fewings stopped, turned and said in a low voice

"No, it's chocolate". He walked on.

"Nice one Mr. Bond!" Laura left giggling.

Jacob looked out of the cab's rain streamed window sat the London traffic. Grand offices and famous landmarks gave way to shops and then, in the West End, theatre after theatre.

Jacob's stomach plunged. He thought to himself 'doing a walk-on role at the school play was one thing, but going on to a stage in a top London West End theatre, when you are not supposed to be there, is another'. He leaned to the right as the cab suddenly turned left down an impossibly narrow streetand then right again to what was the stage door.

"You'll be met by this cabbie in this cab and no other" stated Fewings in a very authoritative manner.

"How will we know if we've got the right cabbie?" asked Jacob.

The cabbie, who until now had hardly been seen beyond the glass screen, switched on his intercom and turned slightly in his seat:

"Oh my dear boy, you will have no problem old thing."

It was Grunters. Jacob smiled. "I love an adventure!" Jacob was reassured at this and smiled.

"Thanks old chap," Jacob replied.

"Right let's go" continued Fewings as he marched them out and around the large old theatre to the front. Laura gave each one a ticket as they stood in the centre of the foyer.

"Ok, good luck, I must go now, remember your duty" and with that Fewings left.

Jacob knew that to take a step forward meant committal.

"Come on" he said and they followed him.

Laura looked around. The old theatre was gilded everywhere in gold trim, ancient candelabra, deep crimson carpets, pictures and pen and ink sketches of the rich and famous who had 'trod the boards' in time past. She was just about to open the door to box three, when a large hand grabbed her and stopped them all.

Its owner was an officious looking, rather stern and suspicious man who stooped. His face was long and pointed, nose was crooked, eyes hawk like and long greying hair swept back over his head into a fading grey pony tail.

"And where might you four be going then?" he drawled sarcastically. Laura noticed a 'staff' lanyard hung around his neck.

"We are going to our box" she replied showing a ticket.

"Oh are you then and where did you get those tickets? From someone's pocket no doubt."

Laura gulped; she knew she couldn't prove anything. It was just when he tried to show them the way out that she was inspired.

"Our butler gave them to us and he'll be back soon." Laura knew the first bit was true and the second it rather hopeful. It worked however; there was hesitation in the grim attendant's eyes.

"Your butler?" he asked scrunching up his wrinkled and annoyed face.

"Yes," said Laura "it's your call, but if you are wrong, his Lordship will be most upset."

The manager drew away snarling.

"Pfew" said Nathan.

"Well done Lor" said Jacob slightly begrudgingly.

The Four entered the box. Jacob took his seat.He watched Laura place the bag of costumes underneath her chair. Jacob willed on the time as the buzz of anticipation grew large. Every other customer was in high spirits; the seasoned theatregoers, tourists on coach trips, young students, visitors from overseas, lovers on last minute cheap tickets. And then he thought 'there are four very nervous and frightened children, couped up in their box in a most unlikely dressing room'.

The lights dimmed as the last few latecomers slipped apologetically into seats. The orchestra picked up Laura's spirits, sending her into another world of excitement as she was caught up in the story of oppression and struggle in France. The overture worked its way through and the curtain unveiled the magical scenery. Worries and fears were transported away and forgotten as the musical warmed and gladdened her heart.

In fact, the whole of the first half had entranced them all. It took the reality of house lights and the descending safety curtain to arrest the dream. Laura soon came to and gave out costumes to the boys. Matthew looked up to Laura, eyes wide, which said 'do we have to do this?'

"I know" said Laura "just think, it's one step closer to mum and dad".

Matthew nodded, understanding beyond his six years. Laura planted the mobile phone on a ledge in front of her and checked for the thirtieth time that the mute was on. Very soon the combination of lights, music, stage and song took her fears away again until the flashing light display of the mobile and the soaring music gave them their cue. Laura reached across to each of her brothers and gripped them in firm confidence with a 'we must do this' look.

They filed out of the box, taking care with the door not to make a sound and tip-toed along the corridor to the 'staff only' stairway. They moved quickly and quietly.

"And what are you doing here?" announced a sharp voice. They all swivelled around and were caught. It was the same man. They remained motionless. It took some time before Laura could say:

"We are on stage now and went the wrong way."

"And how many times have you done this?"the crooked nosed man asked. "For you to go wrong? Don't I know you lot?"

"Time to go" shouted Laura and with that they opened the door and ran down the stairs. The Four moved quickly until they reached another door, turning left as instructed and, just in time, found the stage right door. The angry official chased them shouting "stop!" But as Laura opened the door, a pack of children passed and provided their escape route. The menace of the stage manager had taken any stage-fright away from Laura as she led them running headlong onto the stage into the blinding, hot light, mountainous music and the glare of thousands of eyes. She halted the boys. Other actors looked at them, then, remembering her instructions, she signalled to all four to start climbing up and up the barricades.

Several actors passed them singing strongly, miked up, looking askance at these newcomers. Jacob then realised that Matthew had disappeared. Laura and Nathan had made good progress, scaling down the first barricade and weaving across the stage to the second barricade. Jacob had to track back and across. Matthew was nowhere. Further back he went until he saw him, collapsed on the stage just where they had entered. Jacob scrambled down. The audience was absorbed as ever thinking that another of the battle's casualties had been a child. Jacob dragged him back to the barricade and put him on to a lower section. All this blended into the storyline and so Jacob pretended to collapse alongside Matthew having no idea of how to reach the other side. He took comfort in the fact that many other actors were strewn around the stage. The large barricade slowly swung back to its motorized place, back to the wrong side and back to a very angry hook nosed stage manager. Jacob gave up; there was only so much a ten year old boy could do.

As this scene closed, it merged into the next one in true West End style.Several fruit and vegetable sellers with their wheel barrows and carts appeared. Jacob saw his chance; he picked or rather dragged Matthew up and slumped him into a nearby wheelbarrow, pushing an actor out of the way and wheeling him in victory across the entire stage to find himself in the dark refuge of 'stage left'.

"Laura, Nathan." Jacob called. A door creaked open and a small hand beckoned. Jacob

wheeled Matthew further on towards the door
which opened again and the other two helped
Matthew into the room.Jacob could see the
nameplate on the dressing room door; the famous
actor Hal Fox. Inside, a mirror with lights
surrounding it, dominated the room. Open racks
of hangers and costumes lined most of the walls.
Matthew slumped onto a large bean bag and slowly
came to.

"Are you Ok Matt?"asked Laura. He put a
hand to his head and winced in pain. "I climbed
the barricade thing and slipped and knocked my
head."Laura described to him his unlikely journey
across the stage.

The Four huddled in the room, waiting for
their final act.

"We don't actually know anything about this
man do we?" said Jacob. They all looked at each
other and there were nods. "We've brought the
canvas rolled up in Nathan's bag just to give it to a
complete stranger!"

They considered this in silence. Nathan held
the bag against his chest. It seemed to weigh
heavily now, this, the focus of the adventure he
had not chosen.

A huge roar of applause broke out in the
distance.

"The show's over" said Nathan. He could hear running footsteps and voices. He tensed and satwaiting. Many other footsteps came and went and then another set of steps, more distinctive this time, more clipped. The steps stirred something within Nathan. The steps stopped and the door opened slowly.Hesitantly a man walked in, robed in a black flowing cape and costume. He turned and looked at the children.

"So we meet at last" said the stranger. Jacob stared at him. He was scared. There was something not right. After a few moments of silence, he remembered that the code name was needed.

"Have you seen Mr. Figsy Foghorn?" Jacob asked.

Laura looked at Jacob, but knew the question needed asking. The 'guest' was still sweating heavily; make up now dripping and running.It seemed to Laura as if the show had contrived an impromptu finale. Hal Fox had again turned the audience against him that night in his dramatic efforts to undermine the world of the hero. His appearance and manner looked as though the performance had not yet finished. He hesitated, looking each one in the eye, delaying.

"He doesn't know it" whispered Matthew to Nathan.

"Au contraire, you are wrong my friends" he retorted still staring at each one as if he knew them.

"Well what's the answer?" asked Laura.

"Oh yes" he replied "and I'd love to eat a jar of pickled onions."

Laura was relieved and disappointed all at the same time. Nathan shifted nervously.

"Well" Fox continued "we haven't much time," taking a face wipe and removing some rippled and dripping foundation shade. "I have a rather important engagement now and I must get off, may I relieve you of your heavy burden?"

He looked at them impatiently. Laura looked at Nathan and beckoned him reluctantly to bring his bag. The bag was taken off Nathan's back and the canvas located. Nathan handed it over. The quietness of the moment and the final giving away of what had seemed to be an albatross around his neck, was very quick. They all stared at it in his hand as Fox partially unrolled the canvas, checked its contents and then left turning with a swirl of his cape out of the door. The door shut and then a secondary 'click' meant one thing.

"What?" said Jacob "he's locked us in?"

Chapter Twenty-One

"Pursuit"

The Four stood in shocked silence.
"All that for nothing," said Nathan, he looked at the others and slumped on a chair not knowing what to do next.

"But Fewings told us to do this!" said Jacob angrily.

"Yes, well we'd better wait." said Laura.

Outside the theatre on Shaftsbury Avenue, two men ran into the main entrance against the flow of the outpouring theatre goers. To the rear of the building, two more men ran into the stage door at the rear. Both pairs had a very clear objective in mind. The front pair bobbed and weaved their way around guests leaving and staff clearing up after the performance.

The 'rear' pair made their way past stage hands and actors and quickly reached the stars' changing rooms. Within seconds the men had opened the lock to Hal Fox's room. The Four looked up at the sudden opening of the door, fearing the gang and its 'clean up' boys. There in front of them stood Dan Jembos and best of all…

"DAD!" Matthew cried, and ran at him, knocking him to the ground.

"Where were you?" he asked.

"How did you escape?" asked Nathan.

"Where have you been?" asked Jacob.

"Where's mum?" asked Laura.

"Quick," said Dan, "no time" he hurried them out, re-locked the door and then made them all hide back towards the stage, deep in one of the barricades.

"Not this again" muttered Jacob.

No sooner had they disappeared into the now motionless barricades, than the other pair of men came to a speedy halt outside the dressing room. Jacob could hear the wrenching of a door, angry voices and heavy kicks of furniture. He could sense the men prowling around the stage.

Jacob heard the stage being searched in detail andfroze into the shadows and recesses of the large barricade .His heart pumped frantically, sweat dripping down his neck. The men wandered closer.

"Hey how about this thing?" shouted one of the men "here's a control."

The vast barricade began to swing out towards the stage. Dan climbed up towards Jacob and whispered,

"I can see that the swing of the barricade will expose us all, so I'm going to cut this cable. When I do, I will be very weak and will need your help to hold on. You must do this.".

He said this with a grim and desperate determination. Jacob realized that Dan was risking electrocution. Dan pulled off his socks and wrapped them around his knife, reached out to the cable, splitting its plastic casing and pulled out a red wire. He then looked across to Jacob indicating that now was the time. Jacob held extra tight to one of the piled up doors and scrap furniture which made up the barricade. With the other hand he placed his hand close to Dan's jacket, ready to grab it.

"That's right" said Dan "only grab me after I've cut this."

The barricades swung further round until it was only a metre away from exposing all of them.

Dan flashed the knife through the wire and a hiss of sparks flew up. Jacob sensed a thud go through Dan. He hesitated enough not to get the electrical thud, but quickly enough to grab his collar. Dan's head slumped down and went limp. He weighed the equivalent of three large sacks of potatoes. Jacob held on and only just managed to push him back into the barricade.

"What was that?" shouted the other man.

"Ah its bust" replied the operator "Must have fused it," he swore. "Let's try the seats."

Jacob held onto Dan hearing the men walking through the lower audience section. After ten minutes they were gone. Jacob looked up at Dan. He looked dreadful and was sweating profusely, his face paler than pale, eyes bloodshot. He looked twenty years older.

They all emerged. Matthew let go of his father, he was tired. The adrenaline of a West End stage performance firstly to a full house and secondly to an audience of two, grisly customers, was still having its effect. Dan called them together in a little meeting in the centre of the stage.

"Right we must follow the picture. It is evident that the cargo went to a go-between who was not who we thought he was, at least who we thought we could trust."

Matthew butted in, "Does that mean he's a baddy?"

"Absolutely" agreed Dan biting back his frustration.

"How do you mean follow the painting?" asked Nathan "It's gone."

"Yes" replied Dan "but we know where to, don't we?"

"But how will we get in there?? You can't just slip in can you?" said Jacob.

"No" replied Dan "but this is where the Panel comes in quite useful. Dad you come with me for costumes, you four stay here."

The Four stood eerily on the open stage, looking out to the vast auditorium with its steeply shelved, raked tiers of seats. Jacob knew that there was more action to come, he stood still, mentally drawing breath.

"Ok we will meet you front of house…" Dan clicked off his cell phone and walked with Mr. Fielding; both dressed up as french vagabonds clothes and makeup.
"What…?"
"Enough questions Matthew," replied Dan "quickly follow me."
They marched through the empty stalls to the rear of the theatre and down the short flight of steps to the main entrance. As they left, a gleaming Rolls Royce came into view. Hearts leapt as they remembered the luxury car from France. Yet again it was….
"Grunters" exclaimed Jacob as he clambered into the car.
"Oh, er Lord Gruntfuttock" nodded his father to the driver who was beckoning them in. "Have you all been together recently then?" he asked.

"Oh yeah Dad, he's a good chauffeur," answered Matt.

The car pulled effortlessly away from the theatre, merging into the ever present London traffic. Matt looked up at the night lights of theatres, cinemas, cafes, restaurants, nightclubs and neon adverts. When the Rolls Royce entered the Mall he recognised where they were. Far off and lit up was Buckingham Palace.

The Rolls Royce glided around the statue of Queen Victoria and towards the side of the Palace where a young policeman carrying a gun stopped them. The junior policeman looked at them, raised a hand and walked over to the driver's window.

"Sorry Sir" he announced "we're not expecting your vehicle according to my list."

"Ah" replied Grunters full of optimism, "sorry old boy forgot to phone through, we've got some of the cast here from les Misérables who are rather late and missed the other transportation."

The policeman shot his torch through. "Well I can see you seem to have some cast members but you aren't expected in this vehicle and I don't have anyone missing from the list from the theatre sir."

"Ah" Grunters paused. "Oh I see" he said and then after few seconds he burst into a chortle "Ha, ha" he exploded "I forgot to mention. Can you tell his Royal Highness that Gruntfuttock is here and if he doesn't let me in I will scale the railings singing about the german girlfriend he had before he met the Boss. It's <u>Lord</u> Gruntfuttock by the way."

"What is it?" shouted the junior policeman's boss from a small booth.

Matthew watched the junior policeman, who looked really confused, call through on the phone in his booth.He looked around as armed soldiers kept a close watch on the car. It was silent inside, even Gruntfuttock closed his eyes. Matthew thought he was praying. He listened to the policeman's conversation.

"Oi we've a right one here…….. Ok well just to make sure…."

"Yes sir I just want to check this out sorry to bother you….."

"Very sorry to trouble you Colonel, do you know a…….."

"Well your Highness it's a fellow called Lord Gruntfuttock who wants to….."

The phone appeared to explode as the policeman jumped back and put the telephone back on its rest, walked back to the Rolls Royce mightily relieved. The armed guards backed off, indicated where to park, carried out a swift body search and followed everyone into a small annex building where an X ray machine meant further checks and scans. Matt noticed Dan placing a strange looking box in his coat before he took it off and placed it on a tray which then went through the scanner. All was fine but Dan looked relieved.

Matt walked through the scanner and followed the others through a long corridorand up more stairs until he could hear singing and noise from what seemed to be a large function room. The attendants opened one of the doors. He walked in gawping at their uniforms. Dan whispered to him,

"Quick just join in and look like you know the words." Matt yawned he was very tired.

He looked around to see the entire cast of the show who were putting on a special shortened performance for the Royal Family, the Prime Minister and most significantly the French Premier, who he recognised from that day in the Louvre. By now he was used to going with the flow and so ran around with the other children of the cast trying to copy them. In so doing he received some strange and weird looks. He looked across at the arrival of Gruntfuttock and then back to the Duke of Edinburgh who put his head in his hands.

Laura danced randomly and realised that this was clearly a potted version of the musical.She wondered as she randomly mirrored other girls, who had obviously spent their lives at some version of a stage school, 'What am I doing here?' Here she was, pretending to be a character in a world famous musical, in probably the most famous royal dwelling place in the world. She looked across at her father who was now singing really badly in the chorus line and attracting even more strange looks than the children.

She looked for Dan, but there was no sign of him. This was worrying, she could see various palace officials whispering into walkie-talkies and looking at each of them.

'Where was Dan? Where was he? 'she scanned everywhere, but all she could see were the officials, now grouped together, who looked as if they were preparing to extract the newcomers in mid performance.

"Where's Dan?" hissed Laura to Nathan. She knew that they were seconds from being ejected. Ejected! And in front of the Queen! She then noticed something. The cast members looked surprised. Inspector Javert, the villain of the story, made his appearance on time and did perform quite well as one would have expected, the very slight difference that amazed all the crew and newcomers, was that Javert had undergone a small change. No longer was he Hal Fox, he was now Dan Jembos. The Four stood still, also amazed, as he sang pretty well and seemed to know all the words.

Laura quickly remonstrated with the others to resume their roles, rather than gawp as statues.With the appearance of Dan in so prominent a role, and with Her Majesty appearing to enjoy this rather over the top performance, the vultures that Laura perceived as the encircling officials, now had something else to discuss in their radio mikes.

Things appeared to be improving, but almost immediately, her hopes fell again. The real Hal Fox, bursting with thespian anger and rage, roared onto the stage, wearing all that he had left, which appeared to be the outfit of a pauper. The strangest acting phenomenon then took place; a twofold performance where both men sang the same parts, whilst grappling with each other in a furious wrestling match on the temporary stage. Laura looked across at the royal audience who seemed to be enjoying this feat of drama.

The two men grappled with each other fiercely, while the remainder of the cast tried to intervene whilst outwardly pretending that nothing untoward was a occurring.

Nathan rushed to Dan and grabbed at his scabbard which was clipped to his waist but Fox grasped it first.

'The scabbard!' Laura realised. 'Of Course' she thought realising that the officials were now poised to act. Laura mustered the others together, no longer worried about acting.

"Quick we've got to help Dan get the scabbard back".

The five of them ran at Fox. Mr. Fielding grabbed his arms while the other four swarmed over him. Jacob grabbed the scabbard, threw it back to Dan who was recovering from the assault from Fox. Dan waved them over and threw the scabbard back to Nathan who caught it on the run. He slipped off, out of sight and the others followed. Dan ran in the opposite direction pursued by Palace officials. The Four ran wildly down a corridor full of old portraits of previous monarchs. With every other step there was either a heavy suit of armour with medieval weaponry or a fading tapestry. It was a dead end. Jacob wildly scanned for options. The clutter of heavy feet crashing down the corridor indicated certain capture. He thought again how unbelievable the story was. His Father caught up.

"Hello," said a voice from one of the wooden panels "sorry old things, pop in here". He could have kissed him, despite his corpulent jowls and mutton chop whiskers. It was of course.........

"Grunters" exclaimed Jacob.

Grunters hurried them through a gap in the panel just before their pursuers ran past, oblivious to the secret passageway.

"But how?"

Jacob's question was hushed by the now serious Lord Gruntfuttock, who waited a good two minutes to check that the coast was clear before responding.

"Right let's carry on along this passageway, keeping absolutely silent." Everyone walked on tiptoes until, in the darkness, Grunters whispered, "Stop".

They had arrived at a doorway.

"Ok" he continued, "stand back".

He pulled a lever on the right hand side and the sound of a complex series of chains and pulleys, swinging doors and panels meant that they now stood deep inside a library.It was a perfectly circular room.

Nathan looked around at the curved walls groaning with dusty leather bound books, many of which seemed very, very old. The walls swept up to a point where a small window formed the apex of the roof. He felt a reverential silence, as though there was something special about this large and mysterious room. Grunters shut the door behind them and its fit was so good that there was no way of noticing that there was a door there. The room was a sanctuary.

"We will have to wait a moment" said Grunters.

"So how did you know about this?" asked Nathan, the question he'd had on the tip of his tongue for some time.

"Well," started Grunters, "you see, the Duke of Edinburgh and I were old school chums and we both were rather fascinated by woodwork and one thing led to another, especially when he discovered some very old architectural plans for the Palace which seemed to show some blank unused areas or empty corridors. So we thought 'why not create our own chambers!"

Grunters beamed remembering those happy days.

"Look" said Jacob, "I know my history is a bit dodgy but the Duke of Edinburgh wasn't the Duke when he was a boy and he didn't live in Buckingham Palace.".

"Ah well" acknowledged Grunters "that's where the weakness in our plans lay. You see, well, he and I didn't actually get around to it until he married the Queen and moved into the family house so to speak."

"So how many people know about it then?" asked Nathan.

"Er well, only the two of us and now you lot as well. We sort of did it when everyone thought he was on some official duty and well bit by bit here it is. Rather useful in the end don't you think, what?"

"Wow" said Matt in amazement.

"Hmnn" said Laura as she rolled her eyes up, "boys with toys!"

"Er, talking of toys" continued Grunters, "Jacob if you pull out that old copy of a *'Christmas Carol'* by Charles Dickens please". Jacob pulled out what seemed to be a wad or sheaf of old yellowed papers in a large bundle bound by a ribbon around two separate pieces of hard leather. Jacob, fascinated by this, pulled open the old ribbon and opened the now loose collection of fading parchment.

"Grunters" asked Jacob "Why is this handwritten with loads of crossing out?"

"Well it's the one he wrote himself"

"Who?" asked Jacob dimly.

"Dickens of course!" replied Laura. The look on the others faces was quite remarkable.

"Anyway," he continued, "place it back where it was."

Jacob did this having tied it back together and they heard a far off bell ring.

"What was that?" asked Jacob.

"Ah!" said Grunters, "my compatriot and co worker has been called."

A muffled far off sound of footsteps was heard and then stopped. A now familiar rumble of wood and sliding metal revealed a hither to unseen door opening wide just across from where they were standing. Various irregular lines around a large collection of original expedition diaries in a rough serrated pattern emerged and through this temporary doorway strode an old man.

They were all speechless

"Grunters, what the….." exclaimed the old man who cut short his words when he saw the children.

"Ah well, hello old chap, sorry to be a pain and such, however we've got into a bit of a tight spot. I'm sure you'd be interested in our little adventure".

A silence then ensued and they watched the man's face go through some mental contortions as he considered Grunters' appeal with some reluctant exasperation and eventually bade them all to sit down.

"Go on then Grunters, explain yourself," he said. A heavy and weary long fingered hand ran over his wrinkled, furrowed and royal brow.

Chapter Twenty-Two

<u>By Royal Appointment</u>

By the side of the rounded bay window and settled deeply into a series of long, faded leather sofas and armchairs sat Grunters, the Four, Mr. Fielding and the Duke of Edinburgh.

"This may take some time and we think we should tell it in full" announced Grunters as enthusiastically as ever.

"Go ahead then" replied the Duke. "Bearing in mind the fact that you are still trespassing in my home and have breached some major security checks, I'll hear you out. But only because my old school chum is here, mind you, it had better be good."

The Duke opened a sliding panel from the arm of his chair to reveal a button. Once pressed, the button unveiled another hidden item, this time it was a substantial drinks cabinet. The Duke poured himself a drink and one for Grunters. He looked quizzically at Mr. Fielding, who nodded not knowing what was being decanted, and then picked up four orange drink bottles, handing them out to the children. Jacob couldn't believe that he was being served by the Queen's husband.

"Right," the tired Duke announced as he collapsed into his chair. "Let's have it".

Grunters acted as the narrator and skillfully drew in the various people present to illustrate the story.

It was slow to begin with, but minute by minute the tension and level of urgency grew so much that the Duke, who started with dull uninterested-eyes, became more animated and after a while, began to ask for points of clarification.

Time slipped by, but even the late hour did not deter any of those present, except Matthew who had curled up in the deep recess of the sofa and begun to snore.. The reliving of the story took them all, apart from Matthew, to a heightened sense of awareness.

Grunters finally came to a stop and looked earnestly at the Duke who was the now focus of five gazes. Only the deep 'tock tock' of a far off clock and Matthew's slumberous breathing disturbed the tangible silence as the Duke took it all in. He sipped more of his malt whisky and looked deeply into the base of the 350 year-old cut glass tumbler.

"Well I'll be….." pondered the royal husband, who further contemplated and jiggled the residual ice in the heavy bottomed glass.

"So, he's back then?" asked the Duke.

"Who's that?" asked Grunters desperately trying to keep in tune with the Duke's thinking.

"Why, LeClaw of course".

"Do you know him?" asked the incredulous Grunters.

"Oh of course. He was at Gordonston School in Scotland with me. Bit of a weirdo then as well. Did strange things with chemicals and rugby balls…"

"With respect your highness, you," Mr. Fielding hesitated, "you are of mature years, and well, LeClaw has the energy and vigour of well shall we say a much younger man."

"I know what you mean" responded the Duke "I'm an old git and he's running around as fit as a butcher's dog trying to conquer the World. Well he was always a bit eccentric, you know standing around late at night in libraries and all that. Anyway he, last I knew, was into some blood transfusion anti-ageing thing, seems to have worked. Maybe I should have a pint of what he's on!"

He guffawed and finally they all felt at ease.

"Complete nutter of course," the Duke continued "madder than a box of frogs. I know some of my acquaintances are completely bonkers but he, well he is seriously demented. I gather one of his compatriots is performing here in the Palace then! Oh I guess they'll all be gone now. Well it's very late and you young things should be in bed. We need to sort this out tomorrow. I'll get my equerry to deal with things. Well, good night. My man will allow you to slip out of here unnoticed…..bit like the way you got in what!"

Nathan plucked up courage and with a slight bow said

"Er your gracious majestic personship, there's just one thing". He pulled out the scabbard and its precious contents. In all the excitement of the telling they had forgotten the real focus of the story.

"I imagine that this is what all the fuss is about then?" said the Duke as he peered into the scabbard. "I'll stick it into the middle of Shakespeare…All's Well That Ends Well, Ha, Ha!".He slipped the scabbard in between the many old versions of the Bard's plays and touched a copy of Macbeth.

A real door opened and his equerry appeared. He ushered them through more corridors and then out to the car park and Grunters' Rolls Royce. Grunters delayed his departure as he called up his cell phone voicemail.

He clicked shut the phone after a few moments and announced;

"Great news indeed! The Panel has found your Mother and she's been given refuge in a 'safe' house."

The children were overjoyed. So of course was her husband.

"Where is she then?" asked Laura who was now tearful in the relief of knowing her mother was fine.

"Ah" said Grunters "that's why it is a safe house."

"What do you mean? Let's just go there now, where is it?"

"Well safe usually also means we don't know where, the tricky thing is that it's that safe".

"Didn't they give any clue at all?" asked an exasperated Laura.

"Well yes they did but it's so obscure, I don't know what it relates to!"

"Well tell us, she is our mother" argued Laura.

"Well, something to do with the Christmas lights".

"Yeah!" shouted the three awake children together. Mr. Fielding laughed too, relived to know where she was.

"Well are you going to tell me, your driver?" asked the now exasperated Grunters.

"We are going to our cousins in Cheam!"

The cheering lasted sometime. The combination of the thought of being reunited with their mother and the normality of their aunt's family (although Laura mentally paused here, because there was nothing normal about her auntie and uncle) was a tonic bringing happiness and relief. All boarded the car, with Matthew carried in.

Laura shouted "stop" to Grunters as he pulled away.

"Nathan's missing!" Her father opened the door and got out of the car to see his son standing where they had been gathered by a gate. He was hanging on to it and crying deeply.

"What's wrong Nathan?" asked his Father now kneeling and holding his sobbing son.

The tears were streaming down his face like two great rivers. His body writhed in sorrow and profound crying, so much that it was difficult for Nathan to speak and for his Father to understand what was the matter.

"It's …….I wanted to be rid of it for ages. I had to carry it, then gave it to the wrong person, then I had it again, and now it's gone again….I …" The relief of explaining this overwhelmed him as hefelt the broken tension and worry. His father picked him up, only just, as he was solid for an eight year old and put him in the car.

"I know, well done Nathan". The others put a hand to his head in acknowledgement.

Grunters drove the car through central and south London, over the Thames and then through Surrey. Laura warmed to the immense relief of regaining normality (if this really was the right word) at her auntie and uncle's house.

Jacob looked up out of the Rolls Royce, as it slowed outside a small house in Cheam, and pressed the electric window. A shower of sparks burst out of the darkness. High up on a scaffold and complete with platforms full of Christmas lights, he heard an "Excellent!" from high up. Jacob saw his uncle 'Perky'. He knew he was a colourful character, and almost completely bonkers.

Despite it being late august, the entire house was covered; the roof, the windows, on the lawn, on fences, frankly everywhere, with brightly lit Christmas decorations which flashed, beamed, faded and sparkled vividly. In the night-time darkness of late summer, the house was a huge illuminated display and celebration of Christmas. The car's six travellers got out and stood in complete amazement. Even Matthew woke up for this visual display.

"It's uncle Perky!" said Laura in a not entirely surprised tone of voice.

"He's Perky?" asked Grunters in astonishment.

"Well he's called Uncle Stuart but we call him uncle Perky or even Uncle Stupid sometimes," replied Jacob. The man in question climbed down the scaffold and said "Wow" when he clocked the Rolls Royce. He took his monkey wrench and tapped on the scaffold to alert those inside that there were visitors.

"Hey" he shouted. "You've made it back that's great. Mum's inside".

"Great!" exclaimed auntie Rosie who rushed out quickly only to run straight back inside to get her sister.

The front door opened again and the Four's Mother ran out this time. Underneath a huge sleigh pulled by eight Rudolf looking reindeer and urged onwards by a rather fat Father Christmas, they fell in a large clump of arms and blubbering eyes. Out too ran more children. Auntie Rosie's four children were James, Jenny and twin girls Belle and Elsie. A human pack of bodies united, with Grunters looking on.

Eventually everyone peeled off and Auntie Rosie, a lady who spent most of her time in a dressing gown, called out,

"Now come in everyone," while still hugging Laura. It seemed ages ago to Laura since her visit to this house only a fortnight ago.

Auntie Rosie turned to her sister,

"You've just missed cousin Corrine, she was here this afternoon, gave us a lot of info about what's been happening".

"How does she know? Oh well tell me later…" said Mrs. F. Grunters made his excuses and began to leave. It was now very late, but not before Laura asked,

"Grunters, what's happened to Fewings' wife?"

"Oh she was kidnapped by LeClaw a long time ago. Fewings was a secret service agent after he played rugby for England; we think she was locked up in a chateaux somewhere." He hunched his shoulders "Don't know where though."

Laura watched the Rolls Royce glide away into the night. She found a bed and drifted somewhere far, far away. It had been a very, very long day.

Chapter Twenty Three

Mewslade Bay

<u>14th August</u>

On the south coast of England, from a small village, a long and powerful motorboat eased away from its moorings and moved out to sea. It cut through the light swell easily and when its engines were at full throttle, the nose lifted high and proudly over the early morning waves.

Nathan woke to a morning, bright and sunny; the air was full of hope, one of those days that felt full of promise. He felt the sunlight and wafting breeze. He could hear his Auntie Rosie busying herself in the production of racks of toast, armfuls of cereal boxes and jugs upon jugs of milk. Nathan joined the others. Conversations started up between cousins, spouses, everyone catching up with bits of their respective stories.

Nathan looked up the stairs at his uncle Perky who was standing with only his boxer shorts on and his mouth wide open, looking out of his bedroom window. A Harley Davidson motorbike roared down the road, its chrome glinting and flashing in the bright, early morning sunshine. Downstairs, breakfast was truncated with the throaty roar of the large motorbike. Its rider knocked on the front door. James opened it and took a large envelope. The biker turned around silently and walked back to the motorbike, fired it up and roared away.

A swathe was cleared through the breakfast debris as James tore open the package. "It's a single piece of A4 paper folded three times. Oh look, it's a 'consequences' game, the actual one we played at Christmas"... Nathan sensed that this wasominous; he had that cold, tense writhing feeling again in the pit of his stomach.

"Don't worry children, it must have been someone from our side ...I hope" said his mother.

"Yeah but what does it mean?" asked Nathan and James, "especially as we wrote this last Christmas".

After half an hour of experiments, Jacob, Nathan and James became excited; "Hey maybe it's............" and ran out of the room to bring in a large tray and a box of matches. James took the paper with the story on it and placed a lit match underneath the flattened paper just close enough to smoke it without burning. This caused a shriek of worry from Auntie Rosie who couldn't actually get to James quickly enough to prevent the imminent destruction of this vital communication.

"Yes," he said, "look they've used invisible ink. Invisible ink can come from a variety of sources the most common being lemon juice or wee".

"Yes thanks James, too much information I think!" replied Laura.

Through the smoking and browning of the paper, clear white letters were appearing depicting the lines of the real message, which now read:

> *"Meet me at Mewslade Bay at 11.00 today"*
> # G.

"Gorvy!" exclaimed Laura "we haven't heard from him for ages."

"Well, a week actually" answered Nathan "Since we met him in the tree house."

Laura explained who Gorvy was, but didn't mention the Panel and skilfully kept things vague, something her parents approved of.

"Come on" urged James "I'll get the spades".

Bright gorse yellow blooms, purple heathers, butterflies and bees drifted from flower to flower along a windy, pleasant dry valley path cut into steep 'V' shaped slopes. The two families entered the beach from a narrow rocky inlet which required some scrambling down twenty yards of fallen rock to the neck of the sands which opened fan like into a small cove. Backed by the steep cliffs, finger like promontories of rock extended onto the beach, providing the perfect place for drying towels, wet suits and bathers.

Laura lay back in the sun. She soaked up the warm day with its pleasant breezes. The only sounds were the occasional dull thud and following hiss of the breakers, a gull, a cry of laughter from another camp or the clink of glasses. It was serene.She looked at the waves; they were exhilarating, pounding the sand.

She dozed and after a while sat up. There was hardly anyone in sight, just the odd long board surfer, the boys building several hundred sand castles and a fully kitted out scuba diver.

"A scuba diver! What's he doing here and what's that orange launch doing in mid bay?" she said out loud. The scuba diver kept walking, strangely in her direction. When on the beach, his walk was stumbling. Laura's heart sunk when the scuba diver's path carried on precisely towards her camp.

"Who's he?" asked the tall blond James. The camp fell strangely silent.

"It's Gorvy" replied Jacob.

Pulling off his mask, Gorvy announced,

"I thank you for coming to see me today; I just wanted to say a huge thank you for what you've done. I know we haven't got you-know-who yet, but we've been able to seriously weaken his network and machine,"he said wearily. "I guess he will regroup sometime in the future. Now I owe you a huge debt of thanks and hope that you'll come to me for a proper holiday next summer?"

"No adventures then?" questioned Mrs F.

"No adventures….well…" he hesitated and with a cheeky glint in his eye "who knows?!" and laughed out loud.

"Mr. Gorvy?" asked Laura.

"Yes" replied Gorvy.

Laura continued, "Why are you so interested in this LeClaw? It seems like there's more to it than the bad things he has done or might do?"

"Yes you are right, let's say that there is a family connection..."

"Family?!"Auntie Rosie began to question but was silenced by Gorvy's finger.

"Yes indeed, LeClaw is Mr Fielding's great Uncle. He fell out with the family and in a perverse way decided to use you. He was rather abandoned by your great-great uncle and having found you well…." His voice drifted

Laura continued,

"But what is so important about La Joconde – the Mona Lisa? I mean I know it is really famous and worth a lot, but they had to go through so much trouble and risk and expense only to lose it?"

"Ah well" continued Gorvy "someonedecided to write all the coded names of those involved in their secret organization on the back of the canvas. You would of course need to know how to decipher the code but in the public domain..........."

He left the thought in everyone's minds.

"But how do you know?" asked Jacob

"Ah ha" exclaimed Gorvy "so many questions," laughing conclusively.

"But that's it isn't it" said Laura

"What?" replied Gorvy.

"You really want us to know, don't you?"

"Know what?"

"Why the names were put on the back of the picture,"

"You are very clever young lady"

"Less of the young lady" laughed Laura "but yes, you haven't invited us here for nothing."

"Ok well, yes I invited you here because the task isn't complete".

"But it's not our job to complete the task is it?" stated Jacob

"Well no" said Gorvy "but I do think that we will need all of you to help us resolve this," he hesitated "in the end".

"How can we do that, after everything that has happened?!" said Nathan "I don't want to see that picture again".

"No" said Gorvy "I think you have seen an awful lot of it young man!"

Nathan blushed. "Oh but....."

"I'm sorry Nathan, oh most worthy bearer of the great burden! The truth is that these names on the back of the picture, requires someone to work out what the codes mean."

"So how can we get to the names? I mean the Mona Lisa has been placed back in the Louvre hasn't it? I saw it on the news last night" said Laura.

"Yes indeed" Gorvy replied still looking intently at the four Fieldings.

"I mean there's no other way of knowing what are the names or codes on the back. Is there?"

Gorvy looked out to the sea.

"So" continued Nathan, "you want us to find out the names of the Dark Movement because it is in our interest?" Nathan and Jacob looked at each other. Gorvy murmured something inaudible.

"These people, will stop at nothing to hide or protect their identity" he mumbled again. His face grew dark and his eyes stared grimly out away from the others. And then his face relaxed. "I'm sorry, I'm sorry, so rude of me, now where was I?"

"'Er people stopping at nothing" added James who was wrapt by the old man's mystery.

"Oh yes indeed, nothing at all" continued Gorvy "for now the secret is safe, in the Louvre and not many know of the heavy burden written on its back. Safe, yes indeed, as long as it stays there and is not moved as such..."

"But you think that the dark movement will try to get it again?"

"Oh yes indeed" he added "and of course you have all been associated with it rather closely as well."

"But" asked Laura "they cannot know that we would know what was on the back had any significance especially if it was in code?"

"Yes well that's what we hope" suggested Gorvy.

"So what about Hal Fox?"

"Well he is obviously a double agent, we made a mistake there. We recruited him when he was acting, that's how he knew the codes. He must have a motive for siding with LeClaw".

"What, like his name might be on the back of the picture?" asked Nathan

"Indeed! LeClaw contaminated him and drew out his soul".

Everyone surrounding Gorvy grew rather nervous.

"Well as long as it's in the Louvre we're ok then," said Jacob nervously

"Are we?" added Nathan.

"Oh I think so" answered Gorvy, now looking at Jacob and Nathan closely. "I, *think* so". Nathan looked very uncomfortable, so did Jacob.

"Er Mr Gorvy, one more thing" asked Laura. "Mr Gorvy?"

"Eh? Oh sorry what was that?"

"Well, I looked on the internet about the picture and there's one slight tricky little detail. It isn't there."

"Ah I wondered if anyone would realise that." Gorvy replied. "Thought I'd get away with it"

"What?" added Jacob.

"Well you see, you know we've been carrying around a canvas all this time, on the internet it says that the picture was painted on a small piece of wood?"

"Indeed it was" replied Gorvy

"So what we had was a fake?" asked Nathan his face in total amazement.

"Er no, not actually, no most definitely not. Da Vinci painted two, almost identical. This one is kept in case of an accident." Gorvy smiled a smile which implied a very long story behind it. "And yes, not many know about it".

"What about Tom's parents…?" Laura was cut off.

"Now then, you must report to RAF Biggin Hill today at 4pm from where you will be taken to Windsor Castle". Gorvy himself was cut off by hiscell phone ringing. He fumbled in his cream jacket, his face drained of its colour. "Oh dear, dear, dear me" he mumbled again. "Um do excuse me if I just make a call will you?" He walked towards a cliff.

"Oh no" said Laura gravely.

"What Lor?" asked James.

"There, sitting in the orange launch boat in a black wetsuit." The man in question was the last person she could have imagined being there, and the last person she ever wanted to meet again.

"Who's that?" asked James.

"Keep still he hasn't seen us." said Jacob.

"Look what Gorvy's doing…" added Laura.

"What is it?" asked Matthew

"Gorvy is deliberately distracting him." Laura replied

"Who is it?" pleaded James.

Another bleep was heard; this time it was Laura's cell phone which she had hardly used whilst away. It was a text message and she read it aloud.

"Get out of here immediately, he doesn't know you are here I have been compromised, it's me he's found, go, through the caves, go"

Laura peeked over some rocks to see Gorvy deliberately throw a stone at LeClaw. Laura could see that he had distracted the man she didn't want to meet ever again. The man changed his direction, walked to Gorvy and placed a hand on his old shoulder. Gorvy dropped to his knees, clearly in pain from the metal grip, rendering Gorvy unconscious. LeClaw looked up immediately and Laura dipped down before he scanned the beach.

She whispered to the others "Gorvy revealed himself as a decoy; he was distracting him, quick let's go".

"Is that the man with the steel hand?" asked James

"Come on we must go" urged Laura

"I know," said James. "I've explored the caves, Follow Me".

"Look Dad a text," said Laura as they sat safely in the car travelling back.

"My Heroes, it says" offered Laura as she read from her small screen.

Don't be late for your appointment later at 4, oh and scrub up well. We all fooled him didn't we! **G**

Back at the house total chaos ensued.

"Oh Nath" said Jacob.

"Yeah"

"Well the women and girls spent half an hour talking about what to wear."

"Oh yeah I just had a wash".

"And Uncle Stupid had a mid afternoon snooze."

Auntie Rosie came in, looked at Uncle Stupid and sighed, "You'd never think we nearly just met the all time most evil person in the world, would you now!"

Chapter Twenty-Four

<u>"The Visit"</u>

An old man, dressed in a smartly crested uniform, carefully unfolded a flag. His watery eyes and wrinkled smile lit up when it was fully open. He carried the flag as if it were a new born baby. Pride and warmth filled his 82 year old chest. He would retire very soon, in fact later that week and this would be last time he would ever have this privilege. He laid the flag out flat on his table, gently touched it with his old hands, methodically attached it to a hanging thickly braided rope and slowly and pensively hoisted it up for the last time, through an opening in the roof. It fluttered until the full strength of the wind took hold and its golds, yellows and reds shone brightly.

"So" said Jenny, one of the cousins, "Does that mean we can all go to Buckingham Palace?"

"Windsor Castle my dear, I think so," said Auntie Rosie "er I'm in a bit of a fluster, what hat shall I wear?"

"Well Mum, you only own one, you know your mother's old hat, so maybe it's not too complex a decision".

"Nice frock" laughed Uncle Stupid

"Come on everyone," urged Laura. "we've got to get to RAF Biggin Hill for 1600 hrs, like Gorvy said. Right then, have you all done these things? Have we all cleaned and washed?" only the girls replied.

"How about make-up and perfume?"

A sheepish Uncle Stupid replied "Er well I've lost my aftershave so I borrowed some."

"Ok how about ironing then?" There was no reply to this question.

"Has everyone got clothes then?"

"I haven't got a suit" replied her father.

"Ah this might do" shouted Uncle Stupid from his garage.

"Mum, you've been in the loft for two hours".

"Ok, I've now found something in your Auntie's wardrobe. It doesn't fit around the waist but with the help of a belt...?"

Jacob looked at his uncle's attempts to smarten up and smiled at the sight of him pulling his trousers up so that most of his backside was not on display.

Finally at 3.15 Jacob climbed into uncle Stupid's combo pick up van. As they pulled away he noted the open boot, full with the banging and rattling of lawn mowers, saws and chopped off bits of hedging. After getting lost only twice, the party arrived circumspectly at the aerodrome and, after a quick search by guards, they were allowed into the restricted zone.

Jacob was amazed at the size of the Chinook helicopter, a monster double-coptered aircraft. After the safety talk he placed his ear blocks in and then, when everyone was lined up and walking out to meet the enormous helicopter, he put his hands to his head. Its thud, thud, thud was deafening, like some black dragon, grumpy about being woken by such trifling humans. After having walked bent double under the deafening noise of the engine and blades, he climbed in. No plush airline seats were to be found, only minimalist strap seating clipped to the sides of the hull. An alarming looking soldier wearing a crash helmet checked he was belted in. Jacob watched the man clip himself into a caribina to the edge of the open door, give an 'Ok' sign up front and the grumbling metal lizard roared its powerful engine, and 'thump, thumped' its way up and away, covering the ground with amazing swiftness.

Jacob had a clear view all the way as the doorway had been kept open for the journey. Motorways, towns, Legoland theme park passed below them and then appearing in view was a castle. The metal beast began its landing procedure and the journey was over in what seemed like only a few minutes.

"Dad, is that Windsor Castle?" asked Matthew.

Yet more security measures were in place including an X-ray machine again, and all bags were searched with the finest detail. Matthew blushed as his secret stash of sweets, tucked into his trousers, was put on display for all to see. Uncle Stupid's gardening boots needed close examination, but eventually even they passed the concerns of the guards.

Finally, when all checks were complete, Jacob saw a very smartly dressed official wearing an understated pinstripe suit, matching tie, breast pocketed handkerchief and immaculate shirt, crisp and clean, step forward. He shook each one of the group by the hand. With the smoothest voice they had ever heard he said;

"So good to meet all of you! You have had quite a time haven't you? Now then, I trust you enjoyed the journey, so much quicker by Chinook don't you think? Now then," he exclaimed with legs slightly bent and hands on knees, addressing the children. "Do you know who you have come to see?" Each of the eight children looked blank except Laura, Jacob and James who smiled "I see three of you have an idea?"

"Er" said Laura "the Queen's flag is flying on the pole so I guess it is her."

"Her!" he exclaimed…"Being the monarch of this country, who has reigned for over 50 years through thick and thin our royal Queen indeed!" he continued. "Her line f history dates back to Henry VIII and William the Conqueror."

At this description, most of the children looked at each other, the mothers looked instinctively at the nearby mirror for final hair checks and the fathers ensured shirts were tucked in, not to mention zips zipped.

"Well now," he continued "I hear my brother has kept you under his watchful eye?"

"Your brother?" asked Jacob.

"Oh yes he has a little place in south France, lovely place, nice tree house too".

Jacob opened his mouth widely to say who he thought his brother was, only for his dad to cover it with a hand and smile in an 'I know and you know but don't say it' sort of way.

"Anyway I digress," continued the official, "let me introduce myself, my name is Colonel Fotherington Artworth and I shall be escorting you and introducing you to her Majesty theQueen."

Laura felt a very slight sense of unease about this man. She could not work out why, except that he kept his hands either tucked within his blazer pockets or behind his back. 'But then, that's no clue to anything' she thought.

The group walked out of the building and got into three shiny black Range Rovers. The luxury cars swept away into Windsor town and straight to the Castle. There was no challenge from the police or officials on duty, as the cars were expected. The three cars confidently drove into the cobbled central courtyard and stopped in neat precision side by side. The Colonel marched them into the Castle, passing waiting armed soldiers, police and other officials and into the world famous St. George's Chapel. Laura looked around, aware of its history, which the Colonel then began to describe. She listened as he talked of the history of the chapel including the many weddings and funerals of famous monarchs down the ages, as well as the recent fire.

A strange smell now started to waft across the chapel. Initially Jacob and James scrunched his nose up and then so did the adults. Silent accusations were sent from one to the other and there was much shaking of heads until everyone looked at Uncle Stupid who ignored it all and instead stared hopefully at the ceiling.

"Is everyone ready?" asked the Colonel "right well the protocol is to address the Queen as 'your Majesty' in the first instance and then as 'Maam' on subsequent occasions".

Matthew enquired "What's a protocol?"

The Colonel bent down and said,

"Well it's a posh word for how to behave with very important people" he continued "and of course you do not ask the Queen any direct questions, nor do you turn your back to her Majesty. Is that quite understood?"

Matthew gulped and nodded, the Colonel looked at his watch, adjusted his tie, uncle Stupid tucked in the bit of his shirt that was sticking out of his flies, then the official, who had been standing at the far door, coughed. The Colonel looked at him and nodded and looked at all of them in a 'here we are' sort of way. The official opened the large doors and in stepped an old lady. Laura noticed that she was wearing a pale duck egg suit with matching hand bag. She walked slowly but serenely towards the group and stopped just in front of them.

"Your Majesty, may I introduce the Fielding family"announced the Colonel and with this he gestured to each one.

"And the MacFarlane family".

Laura watched the Queen shake each person by the hand, stopping briefly to personally talk to each one of them. She seemed to know a lot about the story. The Queen bent down to shake Matthew's hand "Well done young man, I hear you have been very brave."

Matthew stood transfixed, "Er Ok" he stammered and then remembered "your Majesty".

The Queen worked her way along the line talking in a low voice yet purposefully. Stopping at Jacob she said;

"And you are Jacob?"

"Yes your Maamship er Majesty" at this all the children and the dads clenched their lips in desperation, trying hard not to giggle.

The Queen continued this time speaking to both Laura and Jacob.

"I hear you and your sister have had to shoulder a heavy weight of responsibility, well done, well done indeed. May I thank you for serving your country so well." The Queen now shook Laura's hand and continued,
"Leading your brothers without your parents in such trying circumstances was most heroic."

The Queen now stopped in front of Nathan and she smiled,

"Ah, so I meet the bearer of the great treasure. My husband has now made arrangements to return it to its rightful owner; no doubt it must have been a great burden for you well done! Well done indeed!"

The Queen bent down a little and whispered "I don't know what all the fuss is about myself, I find her rather plain!"

"Thank you your most majesty" said Nathan and then went bright red at his stumbling words.

Laura watched the Queen move towards Uncle Stupid and noticed how she looked across to the Colonel who immediately looked down a little awkwardly; the Queen looked back and smiled politely. Nathan whispered to Matthew in his ear

"Uncle Stupid is dozing".

After having met all those assembled, the Queen took a few footsteps back and composed herself to give a short speech. Her tone changed and Laura thought it felt like Christmas Day, listening to the royal broadcast.

"I am most grateful for all your efforts, most grateful indeed. You have served your country most nobly and without personal gain for which I am truly thankful. Unfortunately this matter needs to be kept an absolute secret and whilst I understand there may be some loose ends still to be attended to, you have done very well."

She then looked at each one of them in the eye and smiled a wide grin. The smile faded and a serious look resumed.

"I congratulate you all, farewell and goodbye".

With that the Queen was accompanied by the Colonel who now seemed to be whispering urgent business with her on their way out. Laura thought 'he must be a very influential person to have such close contact to the Queen.' She pondered this until she noticed why he had been keeping his hands folded mainly behind his back. One hand was missing a finger.

The families left walking towards the main section of the Chapel, calling Laura to follow them and bringing her out of her deep thoughts. The doorman closed his door and resumed his place outside it.

She could almost feel the quietness which filled the chapel. She looked up, noticing the ceiling's lattice cross-vaulting, the chequered black and white diamond patterned tiled floor and the far off lit candles. The choir had begun to sing for a service which had just begun. She recognised Handel's Hallelujah Chorus, its ascending harmonies and layered patterns kept her standing there absorbing the moment as the ornate melody of 'Amens' echoed around the old stone building.

Finally a burly policeman in a large and luminous jacket stepped forward and asked. "If you don't mind now, would you step this way please young lady."

'There it was again' she thought and walked back to the others.

"Well," said uncle Stupid "another classic chilli con carne meal..." as he ladled out huge dollops

"The red hot chillies........" gasped Matt and eventually all eight children joined him as they sprinted to the sink for mouth cooling water.

"Did I over do it?" asked Uncle Stupid.

"Ah well" said Mrs. F. taking another gulp of cooling water, "that's that then. I can't believe we met the Queen today."

"Maybe," said Jacob "maybe she can't believe she met us today. Especially Uncle Stupid"

And they all fell about laughing till it hurt.

"Dad, Dad!" said Jacob and James both giggling uncontrollably "you know that colonel, well if you use his initials and................

"Yes" replied both their fathers together "we know!"

Chapter Twenty-Five

<u>Homeward bound</u>

"Let not your mind run on what you lack as much as what you have already. "

<u>16th August</u>

The following morning a large recovery truck and driver appeared outside the front of auntie Rosie's house.

"It's the car, it's been delivered back" shouted Matthew.

It was Jacob's birthday and the complete lack of presents and cards was laughed off by all including Jacob.

"You don't need a present" said Uncle Stupid "leaving France is a present for you I bet!

"I guess you're right" he answered.

Laura gathered her bags from underneath the cats that had all taken to sitting on her belongings, climbed into the car and relaxed. The car seemed reassuringly domestic, reassuringly boring and reassuringly peaceful. Waves, goodbyes and 'see you soons' were all said and the car pulled away.

"Hale and Fare ye well" shouted Uncle Stupid waving madly and jumping up and down.

"Oh no" said Laura.

"What?" asked Matthew.

"It's uncle Stupid he hasn't put his glasses on and is looking straight at the neighbour, that old lady there, I think she was going to post a letter, but she's run straight back in her house!"

The imperiously high second Seven Crossing transported them across from England to Wales where signs of the red dragon proliferated almost everywhere, van signs, welcome signs and county signs. Throughout the journey, Laura's mind wandered far and wide. She drew out the old leather booklet and opened another poem and read;

Today I made a field
It wasn't there before
Some towering nettles that sting your heels
Brambles gone, we can play and run, explore
Have parties, friends, adventures galore
Just like an Enid Blyton day and more
From ramshackle stinging waste and rubble
Is a field of dreams (and quite a bit of stubble).

She wondered to herself 'Where was Tom now? Where was Hal Fox? And that Colonel at Windsor Castle....he couldn't be could he?' The miles of the motorway slipped by, as if in a trance, her adventures in France were revisited, questions mulled over and finally let slip into dreams.

Laura woke to the sight of the front lawn billowing in waves of seed heads as the late August wind blew the longer grass blades here and there. Long dandelion flowers also waved, having enjoyed a fortnight of unshaven sprouting. Everything seemed so quiet and still.

The neighbours opposite, Dean and Suzanna were painting their front door and garden fence, for what seemed to Laura to be the fourth time that year. Then to one side, neighbours Len and Mindy were polishing their prize VW beetle and on the other Jim and Maggie were planting shrubs. All waved too. Stumbling and staggering out of her drowsiness she walked into her house. Mindy came bounding over clutching a carton of milk.

"Oh hello, so good to see you back. Did you have a good time, I bet you had some really good adventures didn't you?" she asked beaming.

All six of them looked at each other and Jacob replied,

"Well you could say that, but on the whole quite quiet really!"

The back garden beckoned and Laura sat on the old log which she remembered had been chain sawed into a bench by an old family friend Mr. McDermott, one of the original guests at the Christmas party that had started the whole crazy adventure. Jacob walked into the garden clutching in his hands a large pile of unread post that he had swept up from the hall floor. He joined his parents as they enjoyed a rest after the long journey.

"Do you want the post?" he asked.

"No son, you open it and tell me what I've been missing". His father said quite uninterested in the prospect of returning to reality.

"Well", started Jacob "there's a gas bill, some double-glazing adverts, credit card promotions, adverts for many things you don't need, oh and a letter from the Rumbling-Pearse's…. Jon and Jo and Isabelle and Ralph."

"Oh yes" said his father "does Izzy miss you so much then?!"

"Dad!" said an annoyed Jacob.

"Ok sorry, what do they want?"

"Ah" said Jacob "well they have invited us to see them at October half-term, to go on holiday for a week. Dad they've got that barn conversion haven't they, and two horses we could ride on and two cats and two guinea pigs, Dilly the Dalmatian and those fields with the snow?"

This long recollection was echoed by Laura and her brothers who implored their parents to go. Mr Fielding looked across to his wife who smiled and nodded. Laura thought about the journey to the northeast of England high up on the North

York Moors, it sounded just the tonic for the last few weeks.

"Yes" said Jacob "oh and it says here that Isabel will need help with her homework for an alternative ending to the Pied Piper of Hamelin!"

"Ah yes, the Pied Piper of Hamelin" recounted his father "I remember that story, yes he got rid of the rats but the townsfolk wouldn't pay him so he piped the kids away."

"But what happened to them then?" asked Nathan

"Ah" he responded "maybe we can help Isabel conclude that mystery." His wife looked up

"Don't ever think you can write any stories my dear".

"Any more post?"

"Oh a postcard from Auntie Corrine, from Paris!" replied Jacob.

Laura looked up.

Hot tea and cold squash was all that could be put together for lunch and no-one really cared. The boys went up to the field on the bank behind the garden, a small patch of ground that their father had cut away from the nettles and brambles earlier the previous year. Football, rugby and cricket and eventually lying down in the now long lush grass filled their afternoon.

Laura unpacked and started to write in her diary some of the things that had happened. She sat on the swing and pondered many unanswered questions and then began to write them down:-

1. Fewings wife was locked up in a chateaux, where?
2. Tom of Dordogne, had that steely look when he mentioned his parents' deaths, were they linked to his decision to work for the Panel?
3. How did ourparents get rescued?
4. LeClaw was at university with the Duke of Edinburgh, what was that all about?
5. The code on the back of La Joconde had all the gang's names, would that mean more trouble for us?
6. Who really was the Pied Piper of Hamelin?

She guessed that now was not the moment to ask.

"And" said her father, guessing what she was doing, "why are there five syllables in Monosyllabic?'

"Oh Dad"

"Or why is abbreviation such a long word?"

"Dad!"

"And Laura, what if there were no more hypothetical questions?"

Laura gave up with him and walked away.

Looking up to the field, Laura felt the breeze catch her long straw coloured hair. So many questions she could not fathom out. Her mind span with the huge responsibility she had taken on. HRH had congratulated her and she mused over THAT visit. Her memories of that moment, the face that was on money, old historic clips from the past had actually said "congratulations" to her. The nightmare of the Eiffel Tower, the prospect of nearly dying, the many times of being hopeless, had all been almost unbearable. In her pocket was the note that James her cousin had found the invisible ink message on the game of consequences. She folded it carefully, put it back and resolved to keep it safe. Her body shivered despite the lazy August warmth. High up on the field, she could hear her brothers still playing football, something she joined in with normally only under great duress. But now it was her escape from these imponderables. So, with amazement from her brothers, she walked up the bank, ran into the field, and with a relieved smile, she kicked the ball and ran the length of the pitch to score.

Laura's mother started the washing machine and then collapsed on a picnic chair sleeping in the sun.Her father strolled down to the corner shop for milk, bread and a copy of the *Penarth Times*. On his return he found another garden chair and settled down to see how his cricket club had been faring over the last few Saturdays. He described the remnants of old stories which were still making headlines and was absorbed by the middle pages that referred to the major incident in Paris.

Laura wondered about the family link to LeClaw.

"My dear" said her father.

"Yes" replied his wife fairly indifferently.

"Oh er Wales beat England at Twickers in a summer match, that Jones fellow the coach looks pretty fierce don't you think?"

"Yes", replied Mrs F without looking at all.

Laura looked up. Sensing that to revisit the adventure would not be a good idea, she looked down again.

"Oh er the cricket club made promotion as well."

"Division four to three no doubt?" his wife replied with bored indifference.

Laura decided to walk back up to the field again. She ambled past the football and the high and heavy blackcurrant burdened hedgerows that bordered it. She picked a few of the full and juicy fruits, then plucked a clump of large dandelion seed heads and with a few puffs, blew them away. The seeds lifted up, caught a gust of wind up over the hedges away from the house, over the fields, over to the sea and carried on due south until she could see them no more.

THE END

The story continues with the "The Legacy".

Other books by the Author

"The Legacy" sequel to "The Four"
…just when you thought family holidays couldn't get
more dramatic……………
Soon to be released

Lightning Source UK Ltd.
Milton Keynes UK
UKOW050346070212

186781UK00001B/14/P